SHE SAID NO

but he crossed the line between passion and violence

Kay D. Rizzo

SHE SAID NO

but he crossed the line between passion and violence

Kay D. Rizzo

Pacific Press Publishing Association
Boise, Idaho
Oshawa, Ontario, Canada

Edited by Jerry D. Thomas
Designed by Dennis Ferree
Cover photo by Stan Sinclair
Typeset in 10/12 Century Schoolbook

Library of Congress Cataloging-in-Publication Data:

Rizzo, Kay D., 1943-
    She said no : but he crossed the line between passion and
violence / Kay D. Rizzo.
        p.   cm.
    ISBN 0-8163-1179-X
    1. Man-woman relationships—United States 2. Women—
United States—Crimes against 3. Acquaintance rape
I. Title.
PS3568. I836S52   1994   93-28923
813'.54—dc20   CIP

94 95 96 97 98 ● 5 4 3 2 1

Contents

Dedication

A message to
my "very" grand nieces and nephew:
"Walk in the light
of God's love."

With much love,
Aunt Kay

Prologue

Sunlight streamed through partially opened Venetian blinds onto the books, papers, and notebooks covering the gray shag carpet. Josh Hanson yawned, rubbed his eyes, reached down, and patted the head of an oversized, shaggy golden retriever asleep beside his daybed.

Craning his neck around, he peeked at the travel alarm on the end table above his head. *7:45! Oh, no! Dr. Powell's anatomy exam at 9:00!* He groaned. *I'll never make it on time.*

Rolling his head from side to side, Josh hoped to dislodge the pain in his neck and back. He sat up and eased his feet over the side of the bed. The throbbing in his head intensified. Running both hands through thick, sun-bleached hair, he twisted his head first one direction, then the other, hoping to lessen the stiffness in his neck and shoulders. *Way to go, Josh. Of all days to oversleep.* He moistened his parched lips. His mouth tasted as if his tongue had been the line of scrimmage for Sunday's Army/Navy game.

Josh planted his elbows firmly on his knees and buried his head in his hands. *This is going to be one horrid day! I don't think I slept three whole hours.*

Nerf nudged Josh's right leg. Josh pushed the dog's snout away. "OK, OK, I'll take you for your morning walk. Just give me a chance to wake up."

The dog whimpered and trotted to the apartment door, then back to Josh's side. Mumbling to himself, Josh shuffled his feet over the carpet, searching for his battered running shoes. He located his right sneaker. When he tried to shove his foot inside, his big toe brushed against a piece of paper. He glanced down and froze.

The envelope. It had been true, all true. The events of the previous night surged through his mind, each one with the force of a renegade killer whale.

He picked up the dreaded envelope and examined it. Nerf nosed in, hoping for a token pat on the head. Josh's eyes traced the carefully formed letters, bringing back memories too painful to recall. "Mr. Joshua Hanson, 12994 East Cliff Drive, Santa Cruz, California."

He removed a sheet of scented blue paper from the envelope. The words swam before his eyes. "Dear Josh, I'm sure you are surprised to receive this letter from me, of all people. I ran into your friend Carl last weekend at the Midwest Collegiates for Christ Crusade in Chicago, and I asked him for your address. He didn't want to give it to me at first, but you know me. I persisted until he gave in.

"I guess it's mean-spirited of me, but I thought you should know that Heather has finally managed to get her life back together *in spite of you!* I guess I just wanted you to hear it from me." The note was signed "René MacKenna."

Renés mischievous brown eyes, her teasing, laughing grin flashed before his eyes. He could still see the cool, springtime sunlight backlighting the fourteen-year-old's warm brown hair as it cascaded down around her shoulders. He recalled how she had followed him and her older sister Heather around campus whenever she and Heather's folks came to the college for a visit. His eyes darkened when he recalled the confusion and disappointment on the young girl's face as she stared at him from across the courtroom.

Fourteen—hmm—she must be twenty by now. Doesn't seem that long ago. Josh sighed heavily and stared at the unexpected note. It was hard to imagine that the little girl with the massive crush could now harbor such bitterness. As if performing a primitive tribal ritual of self-denigration, Josh opened the envelope again and carefully removed the engraved white linen invitation. The words blurred before his eyes as he read the message aloud.

Mr. and Mrs. James MacKenna
and
Mr. and Mrs. Anthony Callente, Sr.,
invite you to witness the marriage
of their children,
Heather Elaine . . .

Heather Elaine MacKenna? No, to him, Heather would always be Mac, the dimpled gamin with golden flecks dancing in her copper brown eyes and fiery flames in her deep auburn hair. It was the unique combination of the eyes and hair that first intrigued him. *No, that's not true,* he thought, because he'd first noticed her in the black-and-white campus mug book. Yet one look was all it took. He vowed to his buddies that, one day, she would be his wife. A familiar ache returned to his chest.

And now? Josh set his jaw and continued reading.

. . . and
Anthony David
on Sunday, October 9,
at two o'clock p.m.
at the Chapel of the Pines,
Route 158, Reading, Pennsylvania.
Reception immediately following.

Crumpling the wedding announcement in his hand, Josh breathed a ragged sigh. "Oh, God, will this nightmare ever end? It's been more than six years!" The pain in his voice surprised even him. Nerf licked Josh's whitened knuckles and whined. Josh patted the worried dog's head.

"It's OK, boy. It's OK. How about you and I go for a run on the beach this morning? Maybe that will help clear the ghosts out of my upstairs closet."

The dog bounded about the room, barking and coaxing his master toward the studio apartment door.

Chapter One:

"Tears and Laughter . . ."

HEATHER

I stared at the words scribbled on the back of the Collegiates for Christ program—*Josh Hanson, 12994 East Cliff Drive, Apt. 4, Santa Cruz, CA*—and choked back the bitter bile rising in my throat. A sudden chill ran through my body, as if an arctic wind had swept across my soul.

"How could you, René?" I screamed, to deaden the pain of seeing his name. "How could you write to him? How could you betray me, your own sister?" I paced to the window, then whirled about to face her. "How long have you been corresponding with him? Maybe you need to learn the hard way too."

I moved toward the bed, where René sat weeping into her bed pillow. "You always did have a massive crush on the creep. Even during the arraignment, I saw you watching him. I can't believe it—my own sister!"

René leapt from the bed and threw herself into my arms. "No, Heather, no. You have it all wrong. I wrote to him, yes, but not for me—for you."

"For me? Why? Why? For the last six years, I've struggled to forget his name, his face, everything about him! And now . . ." I crumbled to the floor beside my sister's bed, wrapping René's bed quilt about my shoulders. *If only I could tunnel deep into the padded darkness and lose myself . . .*

"Oh, Heather . . ." I felt my sister's arms around my

11

shoulders. "I didn't intend for you to ever know about the letter. You know I wouldn't do anything to intentionally hurt you, only him. I sent him one of your wedding announcements so he would hurt, so he would remember and hurt!"

"Oh, grow up, René! What makes you think he'd even care?" I closed my eyes and burrowed deeper into the quilt's downy warmth. During the weeks before the wedding, I'd fooled myself into thinking the painful memory was forever gone. Just seeing his name again brought the nightmare all back. All those years of counseling? For what!

As if it were yesterday, fear gripped me by the throat. Guilt accosted my mind. And doubts, all those "if onlys," rushed through my brain. My lungs tightened . . .

Please! I can't breathe! I've got to get away! I clawed the quilt away from my body and leapt to my feet. I grabbed my car keys from the dressing table, where I had dropped them only minutes earlier. My fingers wrapped around the miniature night stick I'd attached to my ring of keys. Out of the corner of my eye, I caught my haggard reflection in the three-way mirror. A familiar enemy I'd believed to be dead stared at me, her eyes wide with terror. Behind me, I could see my sister sitting on the edge of the bed, weeping. I wanted to scream at her. *Don't you know what you've done?* Oh, God, will this nightmare ever end? If only I could go back to . . .

I ripped a facial tissue from the cardboard container and swiped at the tears streaming down my cheeks. A vision of my upcoming wedding night sprang into my eyes. Terror skittered along my spine. *How can I walk into Tony's arms as his bride? Clean? Chaste? Innocent? I don't remember what it feels like to feel clean and innocent. How can I give myself to him, to any man, for that matter? Maybe it's too soon. Maybe by spring.*

Even as the doubts taunted my mind, I knew another six months, another six years would make little difference. My counselor was right. It was time for me to move on. Yet my fears persisted. I had learned to love again, but could I trust him? Could I be making another horrendous mistake? I'd certainly misjudged Josh.

Coming home to Pennsylvania three weeks before the wedding had seemed like a good idea from the safety of my Hartford, Connecticut, apartment. I remembered the concerned look on Tony's face as he waved goodbye to me from the stoop of my apartment building. We'd considered having a quiet little ceremony, just the two of us, in an Early American chapel on Cape Cod we stumbled across one summer weekend. But for me, a wedding day that didn't include my family would never suffice.

In the weeks previous to going home for the wedding, I pushed my fears aside and concentrated on the quiet talks I'd share with my little sister René and the shopping trips we'd take with Mom. I knew how excited the entire family was about my marrying Tony. Mom and René fell in love with Tony the first time they met. And while he wouldn't admit it, my dad did too. I think they were relieved I'd found someone I could potentially love.

There'd been times during the last six years when I doubted I'd ever trust any man enough to marry. My mother knew this. If it hadn't been for my dad being such a solid constant in my life . . . And Daddy, in spite of everything that happened, still treated me as his little girl—someone to protect, to coddle, to love. Maybe that's what hurt him the most, the guilt of not being able to protect me. No, I couldn't take such an important step without either of them present. And I guess I hoped that by coming home, I would find the major dose of confidence I needed before marrying Tony.

Tony, dear gentle Tony . . . My eyes misted at the thought of his warm brown eyes coaxing me, teasing me out of one of my "blue funks," as he called them. He'd weathered so many of my storms and still loved me. For two years—never demanding, always understanding, always there for me—he'd put up with my unreasonable demands and irrational fears. Even now, days before our wedding, I somehow knew he'd understand if I backed out.

I mean, what kind of guy would wait three weeks before he tried to hold a woman's hand and six weeks before kissing her? Later, when we talked about it, he said that I behaved like a skittish colt, and he didn't want to scare me off. He wasn't far from the truth. Now, we both attribute his incredible patience with me to the presence of God working in our relationship. *So why am I still terrified?*

I love him so much. I really do. How can I help but? Tony knows my dirtiest secrets, yet loves me anyway. I'll never forget the night I told him about Josh. How different his reaction was from Bill's, the only other man I'd dated since Josh.

I met Bill at a church outing six months after leaving college. Eager to put the experience behind me, I accepted his invitation to dinner. From there we began dating steadily over the next few months. One evening after a romantic walk in the moonlight, I mistakenly told him about Josh. I never saw Bill again. A couple years later, I completed my teacher-training credentials and landed a teaching job in Hartford, Connecticut.

That's where I met Tony. His apartment was on the third floor, right over mine. All it took was a few encounters over my loud piano practice, a glance or two in the elevator, a broken grocery bag, and the discovery that he attended the church where I'd just transferred membership. What can I say? He was persistent. And me, I was lonely.

So, when Tony and I started dating, I decided to tell him early on about Josh. This way, if he rejected me, it wouldn't hurt so much. We'd been dating a couple of weeks and decided to drive to Boston on the Fourth of July for the annual waterfront Boston "Pops" concert. We were on the way back to Hartford. As Tony's little Spitfire gobbled up the miles along the interstate, we took turns sharing dating experiences from our past. The purr of the engine and ambiance inside the car provided a strange sense of isolation and intimacy. I'd planned to insert Josh's name, just in passing, but once I started, the horrid tale tumbled out unchecked.

Recognizing the seriousness of the moment, Tony stopped the car at a roadside rest stop in order to give me his full attention. He listened as I raved. Anger finally spent, I sobbed, "So now that you know the worst about me, you can take me home and be on your way."

He gave me one of his crooked grins and took my left hand in his. Gently unclenching my fingers, he traced the lines in the palm of my hand and whispered, "I'll take you home, if that's what you want, but I'm not going anywhere otherwise. I'll be around as long as you want me."

I lifted my reddened eyes to face him. The shadows hid his features from me. "Tony, you may feel that way right now, but later, after you think about what I've told you, you'll change your mind. No man wants damaged merchandise, rummage-sale goods."

He leaned forward to where the moonlight illuminated his face and squeezed my hand suddenly. "Don't ever let me hear you talk about yourself that way again. If anything could make me leave you, it would be lies like that." His eyes snapped with fury, then softened. "You are the most beautiful thing to ever enter my life."

When I opened my mouth to object, he placed a finger across my lips. "I'm not a lovesick school boy. I know quality when I see it, and I know what I want when I see it. And I want you."

I buried my face in the headrest. He gently massaged my upper arm and shoulder while I cried, all the while whispering words of comfort to me.

That was a year ago. And now, I'd come home to Pennsylvania to prepare for our wedding. The invitations had been sent, the church reserved, the cake ordered, the musicians hired. He and his loud and raucous family would be arriving in less than two weeks, expecting to find a radiant and eager bride.

I caught my reflection in the bedroom mirror and shook my head. Radiant? Eager?

I could almost hear his voice scolding me. "Come on, Chopin, get a grip!" He'd begun calling me Chopin, pronouncing it "choppin'," the first time we met. I'd been practicing a difficult passage on the piano in my apartment when he knocked on my door and asked me if I understood the meaning of the term *pianissimo. Oh, Tony, where are you now? I need a dose of your confidence so badly.*

"H-H-Heather." René placed her hands on my shoulder. "I'm so sorry. I wouldn't want to hurt you for anything—honest!"

I whirled about in surprise. I'd almost forgotten my sister was in the room. I threw my arms around her and touched my forehead to hers. "I know, ladybug. I know." I dabbed at her tears. "I'm sorry for the hateful things I said. I know you meant well." I took a deep breath and glanced toward my suitcases still sitting by the door. "I suppose I should unpack."

A wide, forgiving smile filled René's face. "I emptied the top two drawers for you to use while you're here." She hiccuped and reached for a tissue and pointed toward the closet. "I cleared a space for your hanging clothes, all except your gown, of course. Mama put that in the guest-room closet." She hardly paused long enough to breathe. "Wait till you see it. She did a fabulous job. You wouldn't believe the number of beads and sequins she sewed onto the skirt front and bodice!"

Once forgiven, René's natural exuberance returned. "And wait until you see my dress. Mama is absolutely incredible. She made Chris's and Ashley's gowns in one week's time—can you imagine? She would have done the flowergirl's dress also if Missy's mother hadn't volunteered to do it herself."

I took a deep breath and pasted on the broadest smile I could manage. "Well, what are we standing here for? Lead me to these works of art."

René grabbed my hand and dragged me to the room next to hers, where Grandma and Grandpa MacKenna would be staying until after the wedding. She threw open the closet doors to a swirl of lavender and navy organza. My breath caught in my throat. The colors worked just as I'd imagined. I ran my fingers across the sweeping, diaphanous skirts. My sister's peachy complexion would positively glow next to the pastel. And I already knew that the rich midnight blue would complement my friends' coloring as well. For a moment, I almost felt like an eager bride anticipating her big day.

I turned at the sound of a beloved voice behind us. "Well, what do you think?" My mother walked hesitantly to my side.

"Are they what you envisioned?"

My eyes misted with tears. I whirled into her arms. "Oh, yes, they're magnificent. Thank you so much, Mama. You did an incredible job. I love you so much!"

"I'm glad I could do it for you, princess." She squeezed me about the waist. "Are you ready to see your dress?"

I swallowed hard and nodded slowly. I straightened my back. This was the moment. A mixture of dread and excitement played ping-pong with my emotions as I watched her remove a giant plastic hanging bag from the back of the closet. Somewhere in the back of my mind, I could hear my mother rambling on, the way she does whenever she's nervous.

"You can't imagine the trouble I had finding a lace pattern similar to the Alençon lace in the magazine photo you sent. I think René and I searched every fabric store between Harrisburg and Philadelphia. I would have felt better if you'd been here to make the decisions for yourself." My mother hooked the heavy metal hanger hook over the closet door molding and unzipped the bag. "I must admit, I was scared to make the first cut in the bolt of satin. And the lace, I couldn't afford to mess up even one panel. We used every snippet and rosebud possible. Your sister has been such a good sport, suffering through all the fittings."

As my mother drew the satin-and-lace confection from the bag, I could hear my sister's voice but couldn't speak. "It was fun. I loved everything but the straight pins. I was always getting stuck with a straight pin, no matter how still I tried—Heather, are you all right? Heather?"

It's white. It's so white! My hands flew to my mouth. Tears blurred my vision. *I-I-I can't!* I whirled about and stumbled blindly from the room. Somehow I made it down the stairs and out the front door. I ran to my baby-blue Geo I'd parked minutes before in the driveway and opened the door. Then I realized my car keys were still upstairs in René's bedroom.

"Stupid! Stupid! Stupid!" I screamed and pounded my fists on the steering wheel until my wrists were bruised. "You are so stupid to think you could go through with this charade! You shouldn't have let Tony talk you into this. Maybe we could still run off to a justice of the peace." I threw my head back against the headrest and closed my eyes. "And what would that solve? The wedding isn't the problem! It's what comes after!"

I squeezed my eyes shut until I could see concentric circles of light pulsating before me. "Please, God, please help me! I can't go through with it. I just can't!"

Suddenly I heard a rapping on the passenger-side car window. I lifted my head and opened my eyes. It was René.

"Unlock the door!" she demanded, her words mute and meaningless. She pounded again. This time she dangled my key ring from her little finger. "Either you open this door, or I'm going to hide your keys where you'll never find them."

I leaned across the seat and unlatched the lock. She opened the door and hopped in the front seat beside me. "What is going on? Mama's standing in the middle of the guest room, holding your gown and sobbing. She thinks you don't like the dress." The indignation in my sister's voice forced me to listen. "Do you know how many nights she sat up until dawn, while the rest of us slept, sewing on sequins and pearls until the tips of her fingers were raw from the needle stabs? Then she'd eat breakfast with the family and head out for a full day's work."

My fury spent, I leaned back against the headrest once more and closed my eyes. "The dress is beautiful. Tell her there's nothing wrong with the dress. It's me." I blew a strand of hair from my forehead. "I can't wear it."

"You tell her—you can't what?" René's voice rose to a screech.

Patiently, as if explaining the laws of thermodynamics to a six-year-old, I repeated myself. "I can't wear the gown."

"May I ask why?" Her arched eyebrow and tapping foot told me she wouldn't let me off the hook any too easily.

Fine! She wanted rage, I'd give her rage! "That dress strands for everything I'm not!"

René pursed her lips in disgust. "What, pray tell, do you mean by that?"

"Do I have to spell it out for you? It's white—pure white! I'd be a fraud to, to—"

"Tsk!" René shook her head in disgust. "Get real! We're not living in the Victorian era, you know. If virgins were the only ones who wore white satin at their weddings, the wedding-gown industry would go out of business."

"René Alexandra MacKenna!" I stared in surprise at my sister's boldness.

"Well, it's true," she defended.

I snapped my face away from her. "You don't understand how I feel. I always vowed I'd be . . . I'd be . . . oh." I stared out the driver's side window. "It's not fair, that's all."

"So who said life was fair? Grow up. You gotta let go, Heather."

I stared out the window on the amber world of autumn. *How can she be so cruel?*

"And, sister dear, I may not understand how you feel, but I sure as blazes know how Mama's feeling right now. She's done everything she can to make your wedding day special. Do you have any idea just how tough it's been for her during the last six years?" She continued on. "Mom's supported you, cried with you, fought for you, prayed for you, agonized over you, her faith in you never once wavering. Isn't it time you stop wallowing in your own misery and think of someone else for a change? She and Daddy have done everything they can to help you heal."

I gasped. I couldn't believe my little sister's ire.

"All I can say is, Tony must be one fantastic guy to put up with your massive case of self-pity. Isn't it time you stop being a victim and become a survivor?" Her eyes flashed with fury.

At the mention of the word *victim*, I came alive. *All the years of counseling, and she dares to tell me I'm acting like a victim?*

"I am a survivor!" I shouted, my voice shaking with anger. "Until you've gone through everything I've endured, don't you try to tell me how I should behave!"

"Well, someone's got to! It's time you woke up and smelled the coffee, lady! You can't go back to . . . to . . . to being the innocent little girl you were before Josh. But you and you alone can determine what kind of person you want to become in the future. If you keep it up, you're going to become a bitter old lady, hateful and suspicious of everybody."

René's face softened. She reached out to touch my shoulder, but I wrenched away. "Heather, I'm sorry for coming on so strong. You're right. I can't know how you feel." She cleared her throat. "But I do know how much Mama and Daddy have supported you through all of this. And it seems to me it's time you show them a little consideration."

"I can't wear the dress." I hated the whine in my voice.

"Heather Elaine MacKenna, you can be the most selfish, unreasonable . . ." René opened the car door, threw my car keys on the floor, and leapt out in one exasperated move. She bounded up the steps and into the house. The porch screen door slammed behind her.

When had my little sister become so opinionated? Stinging from her censure, I picked up the keyring and fumbled blindly until I found the correct key and inserted it in the ignition. The little four-cylinder engine roared to life. Slipping the gears into reverse, I backed down the driveway. Simultaneously, I turned the wheel, shifted into drive, and stepped down on the accelerator.

Tears coursed down my face. The familiar neighborhood of my youth dissolved into a muddied watercolor. I didn't know where I was going, yet I knew where I'd end up—the Pagoda. From the day I first passed my driver's test, the Pagoda on the hill overlooking my hometown of Reading became the place to which I retreated whenever life became too intense. At least, that's where I went before I dated Josh. After Josh, my paranoia more often overrode my need to be alone.

I turned on the radio full-volume. A jangle of dissident metal and rhythmic drums pulsated off my car's interior walls. I eased into the traffic. As I approached the corner, the light at the next corner turned red. I pulled into the left-hand lane to make the turn toward Mountain Road.

Tony, oh, Tony, I'm so sorry. I don't want to hurt you. But I can't do this. I just can't go through with this. I hiccuped as the light changed. *I didn't mean to hurt you either, Mama.*

Honest. I would never do anything to purposely hurt either you or Daddy. You know that, don't you?

The driver in the car behind me laid on his horn. Shaking myself from my stupor, I maneuvered my car through the city's late-afternoon traffic without further incident. When I reached the base of the hill, I started the long climb to the top. The winding two-lane road forced me to keep my mind on my driving.

I turned off at the first overlook and glanced about nervously. The parking lot was empty. A chill passed through my body; then I forced myself to breathe normally. *It's OK. No one is here.* Slowly, I inched my car forward until the breathtaking Schuylkill River Valley spread out below me. Turning off the engine, I checked the area once again to be sure I was alone, then opened the car door. I grabbed my keys and hopped out of the car. I dropped the keys into my skirt pocket and walked to the edge of the rocky crest. I looked down at the bustling city.

One step forward . . . The old temptation never seemed to be too far away. I shook my head vigorously and retreated to a safe distance from the drop-off. *No, I will not destroy my family by taking my own life. They've suffered enough. Man, they've suffered too much.* I hugged myself and rubbed the goose bumps from my upper arms. Taking two deep breaths, I ambled over to a large boulder safely back from the edge of the cliff, climbed on top, and sat down. I drew my knees up to my chest, wrapped my arms around them, and stared out across the valley.

Autumn in Pennsylvania has always been my favorite time of year—the nip in the air, the golden hue to the sunshine, the zing in the crisp Jonathan apples grown here. I threw my head back and gulped in the fresh brisk breeze sweeping up the side of the mountain. All about me, leaves of gold, amber, and brown gyrated in the wind. The deciduous trees stood exposed to the world, naked among the more secure evergreens. I shuddered.

From my perch on the mountain, I could smell the smoke spiraling up toward me from wood-burning stoves in the houses in the valley. Smokestacks along the river belched white plumes of smoke into the air. Off to the left, apple orchards stretched northeast toward Allentown. In my imagination, I inhaled the aroma of apples ripe for the picking. I leaned back and stared up at the mottled, watery-gray clouds overhead. *Looks like rain,* I thought. Then without warning, Josh's face surfaced in my mind again.

It had been a cloudy afternoon, much like this one, when I first met him. My college roommate and soon-to-be bridesmaid Chris Allen and I were in the student union building playing Foosball with two freshmen guys from Writing 101. Chris and I were outshooting our opponents on every turn. When I scored the winning point, I screeched and leapt into the air.

That's when I noticed the sandy-haired guy over by the soda machine watching me. He smiled and toasted me with his pop can. I blushed and turned my attention back to the Foosball table. I rolled my eyes toward Chris and grinned.

"That's Josh Hanson, a theology major." My roommate edged closer to me. Her voice dropped to a whisper. "He's on the student senate as well as being president of the college's chapter of Collegiates for Christ. And is he ever hot—and available! He just broke up with Jenny Renfro, the girls' club president."

"Hey," one of our opponents snarled, "you two gonna play Foosball or drool over Mr. Stud?"

Chris placed one hand on her hip and glared. "Excuse me?"

"Aw, nothing! I've lost enough for one afternoon anyway." He grabbed his red-and-white high-school letterman's jacket and strolled out the side door. "See ya in class tomorrow."

Arnie, the second guy, shrugged, then glanced at his wristwatch. "Hey, I gotta go too. I wanna get through the cafeteria line early so I can get a good seat in the rec room for 'Monday Night Football.' The Bears are playing. See ya."

My roommate sighed and grabbed her coat from the sofa, where she'd tossed it earlier. "I've had enough too. I think I'll go back to the dorm and take a nap." She slipped on her jacket and peered out the large picture window. "Looks like it's about to rain any minute. Ya comin'?"

"Naw, I think I'll run over to the music building and put in a couple hours' practice. My first juries are before Christmas break. I want to be ready."

Chris laughed. "Ready? That's six weeks away!"

"I have to perform in front of the music faculty. My entire grade for the quarter depends on my performance. I'm scared spitless."

"Give me a break." Chris sauntered to the door and waved. "Sweetheart, you're ready for Carnegie Hall, if you ask me."

"Don't I wish!" I snorted as the door closed behind her. As I zipped up my windbreaker, I couldn't resist glancing once more to see if my admirer was still in the room. He wasn't. I shrugged and hurried out the door.

Gusts of wind whipped the fallen leaves about my ankles as I rushed across campus toward the fine-arts building. The first raindrops started falling as I reached the halfway point between the freshman girls' dormitory and my destination. Within a few steps, I found myself deluged by a genuine midwestern gully washer. I hauled my windbreaker up over my head and broke into a run.

Suddenly, from out of nowhere, a giant black umbrella appeared over my head. I slowed to a walk and glanced over my shoulder into the dimpled smile and twinkling blue eyes of Josh Hanson. Always before I'd laugh when romance writers said their heroine's heart skipped a beat at the sight of Mr. Wonderful. When I saw Josh, mine really did. While some girls dream of a knight in shining armor, my rescuer carried a Pierre Cardin umbrella.

"Hey, red, slow down. Where ya heading?"

Red! Red? So much for knights! I sniffed and accelerated my pace—fast enough to let him know I was irked, yet not so fast that I would lose the protection of his umbrella.

He jogged alongside. "What'd I do? What'd I do?"

"My name is not Red. It has never been, nor will it ever be Red!" I snarled.

Pretending to be stung by the tone of my voice, he dipped

his head. "Sorry. I promise to never, ever, ever call . . ."

Before he finished his apology, we came to a sidewalk intersection. I turned toward the music building. He continued walking straight.

I glanced over my shoulder. "Well, are you coming to the music building with me or not?"

"Huh? What? Where'd you go?" He stopped, looked both directions, then bounded after me.

I laughed and broke into a run for the building's portico. In three strides, his long denim-clad legs covered the short distance between us. After shaking the raindrops from his umbrella, he opened the door for me, and we entered the lobby. A student monitor sat at the front desk, listening to his Walkman radio and doing an assignment.

I wrote my name on the practice-room sign-up sheet, then turned toward Josh. He glanced over my shoulder at the book. "Heather Mac . . . Mac? Mac what?"

I shook my head, pretending to be indignant. "It's all there. Can't you read English? Heather MacKenna." I pointed to the last half of my name. "See? There's a *K*, and an *e* and a—"

"You call that a *K*? What are you training to be, Mac? A medical doctor? If so, you'll find Physician's Signature 121 a snap."

I grinned up in his face and shrugged. "What can I say? Some of us have talent, and some don't."

"All right, you win. What instrument do you play? With a name like Mac, you must play the bagpipes."

"Ah." I adopted my best Scottish brogue. "Ye be joshin' a gel, are ya?"

"Touché. Joshua Sullivan Hanson, at your service. Just call me Josh."

I tipped my head to one side and grinned up at him. "Heather Elaine MacKenna, Mac for short."

"... in the Rain"

JOSH

Mac . . . I never believed in love at first sight until I saw her.

I couldn't get her face out of my mind. The campus mug book came out early my junior year. As usual, the junior and senior theology majors held an impromptu bull session in the dormitory rec room. There, with highlighters and notebooks in hand, we poured over the faces of the new crop of girls on campus. After all, we theo majors knew the unspoken rule at the Christian college we attended—"No peach, no preach." The churches chose married men as intern pastors over single. Even the graduate school I wished to attend was rumored to prefer the more serious married student over an unattached male.

At least for me, this was the year my game plan included meeting and dating the woman who would spend the rest of her life gazing adoringly at me from the second row on the right-hand side of the church each time I preached. The one who would stand by my side as we greeted our parishioners on their way out of church and who would create the perfect environment for the two sons and one daughter I planned for our future. She would, of course, work outside the home until the children came along. Then perhaps, if she were a nurse or a secretary, she would continue working part time. But her main interest would be in our home and in our ministry.

We would date through my senior year, marry during the summer after graduation, spend a year or two as assistant pastor for a small congregation somewhere in Kansas, maybe, then apply to graduate school for my Master of Divinity degree. The three children would come after she helped me through graduate school, of course.

Sounds so calculating and sophomoric from the vantage point of six years and three thousand miles. Yet, in some ways, it made a lot of sense. I guess I was just young enough to believe that one's life could be charted out on graph paper, and stupid enough to try it. Perhaps, if I'd spent more time becoming the man my ideal woman would want to marry . . .

My roommate Carl spotted Heather first. "Here we go! Page fourteen, second row, third picture from the left— Heather MacKenna. Would you take a look at that head of hair? It has to be red!"

We all flipped to page 14. Silence fell on the entire group as we studied the sweet, angelic smile. Even in black and white, the riot of curls haloing Heather's face captivated me. I read the bio beneath her picture—freshman; major: music; hometown: Reading, Pennsylvania. I straightened and tapped the book on the palm of my hand. "This one's mine, fellas."

Brad Shores, a senior, hence more desperate than I, growled, "Who says?"

I threw my hands up in defense. "Hey, ya can't fight fate. I know my destiny. And Heather MacKenna is it."

Brad arched one eyebrow. "At this point, it's open season."

I chuckled aloud. "Hey, if I were you, I wouldn't waste valuable time on a guaranteed loss." I stood up and stretched. "You wait; you'll see. By Thanksgiving break, Heather MacKenna will be well on her way to becoming Mrs. Joshua Hanson." I swaggered from the room accompanied by the hoots and laughter of my friends. I paused when one of the guys called, "Does this mean Jen is on the open market?"

At the door, I resisted the urge to glance back at my friends. Obviously I needed to tie up a few loose ends before I could begin my campaign to win Heather MacKenna's heart. Jennifer Renfro was one definite loose end.

Now, understand, I have always known exactly what I wanted and how to get it. At five years old, I turned my mother's hairbrush into a microphone, after which I sang and preached my way into the hearts of western America, in my imagination, at least. To reach that goal, I knew I needed a clean record. So in high school, when my friends messed around with drugs, booze parties, and sex, I steered clear. Looking back, except for an occasional slip-up, I can see that I did all the right things, but for the wrong reasons.

Choosing to attend a Christian college, I continued my clean lifestyle, as far as the drugs and alcohol were concerned. But sex, well, being a male with the usual overabundance of hormones racing through my body, I found it more difficult to abstain, especially with so many willing participants flitting about campus. Yet none of the casual relationships during my freshman and sophomore years meant anything to me, including Jennifer Renfro, because I knew that somewhere in my future a girl like Heather waited for me.

After I settled my expectations on Heather, I couldn't get her out of my mind, though I didn't make my move on her immediately. I needed time to break it off with Jen. Jennifer and I had been hanging out together, off and on, since the end of our freshman year. I knew she would never do as a minister's wife, even if I could make myself fall in love with her. I told myself that I was just going through my "Delilah" phase before settling down.

While I repeatedly told Jen that I didn't want a serious relationship, I suspect she'd missed the message. To be honest, as I look back on the summer after our sophomore year, I can see that I had been sending mixed signals all along. To me, the hot make-out sessions in her off-campus apartment made for pleasant diversions from world literature classes. To her? Well, I'm not so sure. The apostle Paul says it is a sin to tempt a brother to sin. If that applies to my sisters, I guess I sinned with Jennifer long before we went to bed together.

Speaking of the spiritual, the summer was a disaster. My worships dwindled to the reading of a perfunctory text and a halfhearted prayer before tumbling into bed at night. While I'd never been a dedicated theological student, I figured I had plenty of time for that in graduate school.

During the week before the fall quarter began, things got pretty steamy between us. I'd leave her apartment disgusted with myself and furious with her. Jennifer liked to tease, especially while watching videos together in the evenings. On screen, the actors would be going at it sexually. And on the sofa, Jen would be driving me crazy with the same suggestive little moves, running her fingers up and down my thighs, drawing lazy circles on my bare chest, nibbling on my ear, pressing her incredible body against me.

What could I do but respond in kind? Then, when I couldn't take any more and forced myself on top of her, she'd look up at me through lust-filled eyes and whisper a breathy, "No, Josh, we can't. You're a theology major, remember?"

Talk about a bucket of ice water in the face! Ragged with passion, I'd roll off her, uncertain whether she really wanted me to stop. Then while I struggled to control my temper and regain my composure, she'd pop up off the couch and bounce across the apartment to the telephone. "I'm hungry. Let's order a pizza."

Later, back at the dorm, my friends would needle me to tell them whether I'd scored. Most of the time, I'd tell them to get lost, to mind their own business, or to get a life. But one night, I'd grown tired of the harassment, or maybe I still stung from her snide comment about being a theo major, I don't know. But when Carl, my roommate, implied I'd struck out again, I smirked and arched one eyebrow.

"Excuse me, gentlemen, but I need to take a shower."

Even though I was an upper-division theology major, I didn't think of myself as a prude, nor did I consider myself a lech. Jen and I were getting pretty thick. Knowing she would never become Mrs. Josh Hanson, I let the guys believe what they wanted to believe about our relationship. I guess Dr. Bowers, my theology professor, would call it a sin of omission.

As far as I was concerned, the summer ended just in time. From a spiritual perspective, it had been a disaster. Once the fall-quarter classes began, I cut back on my visits to Jen's place, for with Heather MacKenna dazzling my imagination, my desire to be with Jen drastically diminished.

For the first month of classes, I observed Heather from a distance. The more I watched, the more I liked what I saw. I knew it was risky to wait, but I had to be sure she measured up to my expectations. During the three weeks Heather MacKenna dated a freshman from Wisconsin, I continued dating Jenny. When I heard they split, I decided to make my move. The time had come to break it off with Jenny.

That evening, instead of going to Jenny's apartment, I took her for a drive to a place the college kids called Make-out Point—a small rise overlooking the entire campus. I'd intended to tell her immediately but turned coward when I saw that she'd brought along a picnic supper and a blanket.

We spread the blanket out on a smooth, grassy spot and sat

down. Before I could ask, "What's for lunch?" she was all over me. I mean, she was all over me! At first her aggression disgusted me. Then my hormones replaced my reason. One thing led to another. And, well, this time, after she said No and I attempted to comply, she pulled me back into her arms. And, well, I'm sure you get the picture.

No, wait, I've got to be honest about this. If I've learned anything during the last six years, it's the motto "To thine own self be true." That day at Make-out Point? She didn't hold a knife to my jugular vein. I was a willing participant. I easily outweighed her by sixty pounds. At any time, I could have pushed her away, but I didn't. I excused my actions. *You're only human, man. Don't be a woos. Enjoy! The woman is giving out free samples. Besides, doesn't Jesus Himself say that if you sin in your mind, you might as well go ahead and do it?*

Needless to say, I didn't break up with her that night as planned. That would have been crude. I waited until the following Tuesday. By then, guilt gnawed at me so badly that I hated the sight of her. I arranged to meet her in the cafeteria. I figured she'd keep her control better if I ended it with her in a public place. I was right. I have to give her credit. Jennifer has class. She left the table holding her head high while I felt like a garden slug. Moments later, Heather and a group of her friends entered the cafeteria, and all my guilt over Jennifer faded.

To keep from hurting Jennifer more, I decided to wait out the week before approaching Heather. However, before I could make my move, a sophomore from Florida asked Heather out. Their romance lasted exactly five days. Two days later I saw her and her roommate Chris playing Foosball in the student lounge with two prepubert gym rats. By the way they were drooling over Heather, I knew one of those guys would soon move in if I didn't. Before long, the game broke up, and her friends left.

Knowing she spent time each afternoon in the fine-arts building practicing the piano before going to supper, I rushed ahead of her to the student finance building and lay in wait.

A sudden cloudburst played right into my hands. Spying an abandoned umbrella in the entryway, I grabbed it and ran after her as she passed. By study hall that night, the guys knew Heather "Mac" MacKenna was off-limits to anyone but me. And the rest is history, so they say. Hmm, if only life were really that simple. If only the human factor didn't come along and foul up what appeared to be the perfect plan.

The morning after I received the note and wedding announcement from Heather's little sister, I forgot about my anatomy test. I forgot about my makeup lab. I forgot to go to work. I had no idea what I'd say to the "scourge of the medical faculty." At the rate I was going, I'd be so old, I wouldn't have the strength to attend my own graduation. The university would have to mail my medical degree to the senior citizen's center where I'd be living by then.

Nerf and I ran along the beach until I collapsed face down on a seaweed-draped rock. When I recovered enough to look around, I found myself near the town of Davenport, ten miles north of the small college town where I lived. I climbed atop a large outcropping of rocks and sat down while Nerf chased the tides. The waves crashed against the shoreline, inching ever closer to my perch. Circling over the water, a flock of pelicans searched for food. I watched as the birds spotted their prey, divebombed into the icy Pacific, then bobbed to the surface a few seconds later, clutching their catches in their beaks.

"It's a dog-eat-dog world," I muttered aloud. Nerf bounded to me and lunged at me. I laughed and scratched his head. "I wasn't talking about you, sport."

I climbed off the rock and jogged toward the grassy slope beyond the tide line. I sat down on the grass and cuffed Nerf playfully. We tussled until the dog pinned me down, his two front paws planted triumphantly in the center of my chest, his sandpaper tongue rasping across my day-old beard. I pushed him off me and sat up. "OK, OK, you win. Go catch a sand flea or something."

I picked up an abandoned half-shell and tossed it into the

surf. Nerf retrieved it and laid it at my feet. Then, apparently satisfied with himself, he stretched out on the grass beside me. Idly, I patted his head and returned my attention to the encroaching tide. By now, a new, larger flock of pelicans circled overhead in search of food.

Farther out in the bay, a lone seal fished for his lunch. I watched him dive into the surf, pop up out of the water, and roll over onto his back. From where I sat I could hear him crack the shell of his prey, eat, then clap his hands together with gleeful abandon.

"If only life were that simple, buddy." At the sound of my voice, Nerf scrambled to his feet and licked the salt spray from my face. "Come on, sport, let's head back home."

Nothing had been simple in my life since Mac. Sometimes I felt like I measured my life, not by days, months, or years but by before Mac and after Mac. Before Mac, I knew where I was going, and I knew how to get there. After Mac, all the preconceived notions I had about love and marriage, about my career choices, about men and women in general were shattered by the 9.7 earthquake that left my life in shambles.

Chapter Two:

"I'll Never Be the Same . . ."

HEATHER:

While Dr. Bingham droned on for a solid hour about amoebas and paramecium, I doodled hearts and flowers in my biology notebook. I wrote Josh's and my names together. I printed our names. I wrote our names in calligraphy. If I could have, I would have carved them in granite. But all I had was lined notebook paper. *Josh Joshua Sullivan Hanson Joshua and Heather Josh and Mac Joshua Hanson and Heather MacKenna Mrs. Joshua Hanson Pastor and Mrs. Joshua Hanson Heather Hanson*

It sure messed up my biology notes. I didn't worry that when it came to test time, that awful dead week, I wouldn't be able to make any sense out of them. At least I was consistent. My notes for my other classes weren't any clearer. After dating Josh for only a week, I felt like I'd known him forever.

Looking back, I see that, except for my piano practice, I let most of my classwork slide after meeting Josh. We were together from seven in the morning until midnight, seven days a week, except for classes, of course. However, I drew the line on my practice sessions at the music building. I couldn't allow him to disturb the concentration I needed to prepare for my first juries. I knew if I messed up there, I could be bounced out of the music-performance program, and another eager freshman pianist would gladly slip into my place.

Our first weekend together, my family met him for the first

time. They'd driven out from Pennsylvania for the college amateur hour, since I was competing on the piano. A banjo duet doing a Kentucky bluegrass medley walked away with grand prize, and a piano-performance senior placed first in the instrumental section. Josh's male quartet took first in the vocal group category with a jazzy rendition of "Blue Moon." I was proud to show him off to my parents. And I knew the moment René met him, she was smitten.

After the program, my parents took us to Dairy Delight for ice-cream sundaes. My father, a classical music enthusiast, had been regaling us with his opinion of the cello soloist's strange rendition of "Clair de Lune" and I'd just spooned the last mouthful of vanilla ice cream and hot fudge into my mouth when Josh leaned across the table toward my father and said, "It's too bad what they learned about Beethoven the other day."

My father frowned. "What was that?"

In hushed tones, Josh confided, "They dug up his grave and found him decomposing."

For a moment, my father stared without saying a word while the rest of us laughed, then added, "That was base, my dear boy, truly base."

My sister René giggled. "You're in treble with that one, Dad."

"More like flat," my mom added.

Not to be left out, I grinned over at her. "Sharp, Mom."

Josh winked at me. "Get the point?"

From there, our puns grew increasingly absurd. I leaned back against the Naugahyde booth and smiled. I knew Josh had broken down any resistance my father might have had regarding the man in his little girl's life. My mother's reaction, however, I still wasn't too sure about.

Before my parents left for home on Sunday afternoon, I asked my mother what she thought of Josh. She frowned. "He seems like a nice young man. But be careful, dear; you're very young. Don't rush things."

"What do you mean, rush? We just started dating last week."

"That's just the point." Mom tilted her head to one side. "This man's looking for a life partner, not a casual dating partner. Are you ready to settle down to one guy? You have three more years of college to go."

"Mother, I'm not a child. Josh and I aren't serious. Besides, I know what I want, and I know where I'm going."

She nodded. "You may not be serious, but he is. Mark my word."

Mother and her insights! I heaved an exasperated sigh. She believed that her gift from the Spirit was the gift of discernment. All I knew was I hated it when she had one of them. Maybe it was because they were often regarding me and were, more often than not, accurate. "He's just a friend."

She kissed my cheek and climbed into the car. "Just be careful, sweetheart."

I kissed my dad goodbye, then turned toward my sister. As I kissed her cheek, she whispered, "I think he's totally perfecto! Do you know if he has a younger brother my age?"

I laughed. "I don't think so."

"Rats!" René giggled, hopped in the back seat, and closed the car door. I fought back tears as I watched them drive east toward home. Would it ever get any easier seeing them drive out of my life? I whirled about and ran toward the dormitory. I didn't hear Josh behind me.

"Hi, beautiful. I came over to see if you're going to spend any time at the music building this afternoon. Hey, what's the matter?"

I swiped at a runaway tear. "My folks just left."

He smiled and put his arm protectively around my shoulders. "You're going to see them in a few weeks, at Thanksgiving break, you know."

I sniffed and allowed him to lead me toward the fine-arts building. "I know. I'm being silly, I guess."

He laughed. "I like tenderness in my woman. So did I pass the test?"

I looked up at him in surprise. "Test? What test?"

"Did your folks accept me as their future son-in-law?"

"Their what?" I pulled away from him in surprise.

"Their future son-in-law." He cast a matter-of-fact grin my way.

"Excuse me? We've been dating less than two weeks."

"So?" He shrugged. "What can I say? I know a good thing when I see one."

"And I know a sweet-talkin' con man when I see one too." I jabbed him in the ribs. He laughed and changed the subject.

Over the next week, Josh managed to conveniently show up at the end of my afternoon practice time each day. On Friday, he kissed me. I'd just mastered a difficult Bartók number when he arrived to take me to supper. I was elated with my success.

I glanced over my shoulder as the door opened. A smiling Josh peeked around the corner. "Hi."

Excited over my accomplishment, I leapt from the piano into his startled arms. "Oh, Josh, I can't believe it!" I squealed, giving him an unexpected hug. "I played the third movement straight through from memory with no breaks and no awkward pauses. Straight through!"

He didn't respond. Instead, he gazed into my eyes with that glassy look guys get when they're thinking about kissing you. He tilted my chin upward. My breath caught in my throat as he studied my lips, all the while inching closer to them. Wanting it as much as he, I leaned into the kiss.

Our relationship accelerated after that first kiss. While I still insisted on the sanctity of my daily piano-practice sessions, we found the practice studio a convenient place to be together without interruptions. I enjoyed these private times together. He'd sit on the floor and study his Greek while I hammered out the classics. After putting my time in at the keyboard, we'd make out for a while before going to the cafeteria for supper.

Make out—I always hated that term. It sounds so self-seeking. But it wasn't like that for us. In those first few weeks, Josh was a gentleman. Unlike so many guys I'd dated, he didn't try to push me farther than I was willing to go.

Because of Josh's popularity and involvement in campus activities, people were always seeking him out. He had charisma. People gravitated to him, all eager to bask in his popularity. Being a mere freshman, I enjoyed wearing the title of "Josh's girl." I went out of my way to please him.

Over Thanksgiving break, he went home with his roommate Carl to Michigan. Carl and he had planned a snowmobile outing in northern Ontario. After my last class, Josh drove me to the airport to catch my flight. He kissed me goodbye at the jet way. The way the other passengers glanced at us, I felt like a heroine in an old World War II movie. The glow lasted all the way to Philadelphia, where my dad met my plane.

At home, it seemed every sentence I uttered included Josh's name. I knew this disturbed my mother, even though she didn't say anything. Even my father commented on the frequency with which Josh entered our holiday conversation. I tried to talk about other things, especially when Grandmama was there. But whenever I wasn't talking about Josh, I was thinking about him. I couldn't understand my mother. All her talk about finishing my degree. I mean, didn't she want her daughters to fall in love and marry? And wasn't college the place for that? After all, I could teach piano lessons with or without a degree.

Of course, my sister didn't make it any easier—she and her incessant questions. She was in love, madly, fiercely, undeniably in love with him. She couldn't hear enough about him. Alone in our room the first night, she demanded to know every detail of our courtship. "So, did he kiss you goodbye?"

"Yes . . ."

"Was it a passionate kiss?"

"Yes . . ."

"Did he do it in front of everyone?"

"Yes . . ."

René sprang across the gulf between our beds. "Stop it! I can't stand it! Tell me everything!"

I laughed. "There's nothing to tell, really."

My little sister groaned. "Right, and pigs fly. Spill it! When did he first kiss you? Was it romantic?"

"René, I shouldn't be telling you this. After all, you're too young for such nonsense!"

"Get real! It's not as if I've never been kissed, you know."

I laughed. "Sweetheart, trust me. There's no comparison between the guys I dated in high school and Josh. They're just not in the same league." I wrapped a comforter around my shoulders and expounded on the attributes of Joshua S. Hanson, perfection personified.

Thanksgiving break flew by at record speed, yet seemed interminable. I didn't fool anyone. My eagerness to return to campus spilled out, no matter how much I tried to contain it. As I said goodbye to my family at the jet way, I reminded my mother I'd be home in three weeks' time for Christmas. She nodded, a sad smile touching the corners of her mouth.

"Three weeks can be a lifetime, child."

I kissed her on the cheek. "Don't worry so much, Mama. I'll be just fine. I know what I'm doing."

She caught my face between her two hands. "Heather, be careful. Make sure God is leading with you and Joshua. Pray for guidance and wisdom."

I gently removed her hands with mine. "I will, Mama, I promise."

I kissed my father once again, waved, and skipped down the jet way to catch up with the last of the passengers to board.

Once airborne, concern about parents and home vanished, superseded by thoughts of Josh. He met me at the airport with a dozen red roses and open arms. On the way back to campus, we parked and made out for a while. It felt so good being in his arms again. When the windows steamed over and we were both dangerously short of breath, we decided to call it quits for the night.

One afternoon, he arrived at the practice studio near the end of my two-hour rehearsal. He placed his hands on my shoulders and kissed me on the back of the neck. I remember I was wearing a pleated, red wool plaid skirt and the loose white silk top I always wore under my wool sweaters so I wouldn't itch. When I'd arrived at the practice studio, I'd removed the fisherman knit pullover sweater my grandmother had made for me and tossed it onto the folding chair in the corner of the practice room.

Goose bumps skittered up my spine as Josh absently ran his hands over my shoulders and arms. Taking a piece of sheet music from his hip pocket, he placed it on the piano in front of me and asked if I'd accompany him on a difficult solo number he was doing for the college vespers program. I smiled up at him adoringly.

After going through the number together a couple of times, I played the resolving chord triumphantly. "I think we have it, don't you?"

Lifting my hands from the keyboard, Josh drew me around to face him, slowly lifting me into his arms. "That's enough rehearsing for one day." He kissed me once, twice, three times. He dotted my face and neck with tiny, moist kisses. As his kisses grew more insistent, I responded with like passion. From there, things heated up quickly. At first, I didn't notice when his hands slipped under the silk blouse and began scaling up my back. Truthfully, maybe I didn't want to notice—I don't know. However, my mind snapped on red alert when he unhooked my bra. I squirmed in his arms. My lips brushed against his neck; my words came in short, uncertain gasps. "No, Josh, no."

Rather than releasing me, his right hand slid around to my stomach and up the front of my blouse. I pushed on his chest. "No, Josh, not here! Not now! Please, I . . ."

He uttered a low growl and slid his hand out from under my blouse and crushed me to him. I couldn't move. Warning bells jangled in my brain. Being imprisoned in his arms scared me. I turned my face away. "No, Josh, I mean it. I don't want to go any farther."

"You shouldn't tease a guy like that, you know." He gave me a punishing kiss. I could taste blood. Suddenly, he shoved me away and pounded his fist into the wall. "I hate it when girls play their stupid games!"

My hands flew to my blazing cheeks. "I'm sorry. I didn't mean to lead you on, honest."

"Well, that's what you did! There's a point when a man can't stop just because the girl gets squeamish!"

I whirled about to face him. I'd seldom seen Josh irritated, since most people went out of their way to please him, including me. Yet, his accusation infuriated me. "Really! If you ask me, you're just angry because you didn't get your way."

"I'm a man!" he shouted, with the force of Helen Reddy singing, "I am woman; hear me roar!"

"So I've noticed." Disgusted, I grabbed my music books, sweater, and coat and stormed from the room. He followed me to my locker. Remaining aloof, like a petulant five-year-old denied a second ice-cream cone, he helped me on with my coat and walked me to supper. We never talked about the altercation, but I sensed the battle was far from over.

Don't get me wrong; I like cuddling and kissing as much as any female, but long ago, I vowed I'd be a virgin when I married. I know it sounds crazy to some people, but I wanted to give my future husband my all, and I expected the same from him. I mean, why settle for yard-sale merchandise when designer, one of a kind, is available? Right? Besides, I believed that was what God wanted too. How could a relationship have His blessing if the couple involved didn't respect God's laws? How could they ask for directions in their romance when they'd already rejected the advice found in His Word?

Sometimes, during high school, it had been tough. Maybe grade-school kids could spout the "Just say No" slogan, but in high school? Well, let's just say it was tough. My girlfriends could handle my wanting to wait until I was married before having sex with a guy. But my expectations that my husband remain pure brought taunts. Gwen, the loudmouth of the group, decided I would probably end up joining some Tibetan monastery, since none of the guys we knew would admit to still being virgins. Reminding them that women entered convents, not monasteries, didn't lessen their laughter.

One on one, each of my friends admitted she wished she'd waited or that she was waiting too, but didn't have the courage to say so when we were all together. My friend Judi, for example, once confided to me that she admired my decision. She said that she wished she'd waited. As to what my dates thought, who could tell?

I remember one guy in particular. His name was Carter, Carter Lewis. We'd dated probably three times. And I guess for him *3* was the magic number, because after the football game at the school, we grabbed a bite at a burger joint and drove up to the Pagoda in his Honda Civic. He'd barely killed the engine when his hands were all over me. Somehow I knew how a car must feel when it's run through a car wash.

I pushed him away. He came at me again.

"No! Carter, I mean it." I shrank from his fingers caressing my neck.

"Aw, come on, baby, don't be an ice princess. The other girls—"

With great deliberation, I removed his hand from my neck. "I don't care about the other girls. I'm me. And I'm telling you No."

Carter's petulance shifted to arrogance. He snorted derisively. "Heather, I thought you were cool. Certainly you are aware that ninety-five percent of women, when they marry, are not virgins, aren't you?"

I lifted one eyebrow and sneered. "Well, praise be to the fabulous five!"

Carter revved the car engine. "Boy, I feel sorry for your man, if you ever find one."

I looked down my nose at the toad. "Trust me, Carter. If I had to settle for the likes of you, I'd as soon dedicate my body to science." Folding my arms across my chest, I stared straight ahead. "Take me home!"

I never dated Carter again. He tried to spread stories about me around campus, but all of my friends knew what a jerk he was and didn't believe him. While the names and faces of my dates changed, the evenings, all too often, ended the same, in a wrestling match. What bothered me most about Josh and my encounter in the practice studio was that it all felt too familiar. All too much like the bouts I remembered from earlier days. I wrestled with conflicting emotions of guilt, anger, pleasure, and shame. Maybe my high-school friends were right. Maybe my dreams were unrealistic. Maybe I did expect too much from a man.

No, I decided, *I have a right to decide what kind of person I want to be. And no one, not even Josh, has the right to take that away from me!*

Josh remained aloof for a couple of days. When I tried to explain myself to him, he refused to discuss it. I tried to coax him out of his bad temper, but couldn't. Our cold war continued until dead week, the week before quarter finals.

That was the week a heavy snow fell. The student body awakened to a fantasy world of snow and icicles. Along with the unexpected snowstorm, a pipe in the main administration building broke. At breakfast, the dean of academic affairs announced that the school administration had suspended all first-period classes. Josh and I lingered over our breakfast, sipping on second cups of hot chocolate until everyone else had left. Noting that the cafeteria staff glared each time they passed our table, we decided to leave. We ambled out of the cafeteria into a massive free-for-all snowball fight.

Having grown up in Pennsylvania snow country, I knew the best line of defense was a good offense. I grabbed a handful of snow, threw it at the first person I saw, and headed for cover behind the nearest box shrub. Josh, a California boy, paused long enough for Brad, one of his friends, to take aim and fire a direct hit. *Smoosh,* right in the face! Josh charged in the direction of the snowball. That was the last I saw of him.

A vicious battle followed. Since there were no sides, I don't know who was winning. Kevin Bennett, a quarterback on the college's varsity football team, lobbed a snowball across the commons at my roommate. Chris screamed. His aim was as good off the gridiron as it was on. His laughter echoed off the red brick building.

Why you . . . I couldn't let him get away with that. Sneaking out from my hiding place, I tiptoed up behind him and dumped a basketball-sized clump of snow down his neck. Before I could retreat to safety, his long arm wrapped around my waist, and I felt myself lifted off my feet.

"Just where do you think you're going, little lady?" he shouted.

"I'm not a little lady." I kicked and screamed. "Let me go!"

"Not until I wash your face in a snowbank." He laughed as my arms and legs flailed the air. He tossed me into the nearest snowbank. Coming to my rescue, Chris shouted and heaved a snowball at him. Kevin ducked, lost his footing, and fell face down on top of me with such force that it knocked the wind out of both of us. For a second, we stared at each other, too stunned to move.

I was the first to recover. Completely pinned, I moved the only part of my body still free, my mouth. "Get off me, you big oaf!"

The oversized PE major reddened. "Oh, excuse me. I'm sorry. Are you all right? I didn't mean to . . ."

"Just get off of me, please."

Before he could respond, someone else fired another gigantic clump of snow, catching Kevin at the back of the neck. Shaking the loose snow from his shoulders, he rolled off me and helped me to my feet. I shook the snow from my tangled hair while he apologized once again.

"Here, let me help you." He brushed at the snow on my back and shoulders. In his eagerness to help, his gloved hands brushed at the snow sticking to the front of my ski jacket. Startled by the contact, I put my hand on his.

"That's OK. Thanks, I can handle it from here."

When he realized his hand was resting on a particularly sensitive part of my anatomy, his face flamed with embarrassment. Instantly, he yanked his offending hand away as if he'd been scorched by a hot branding iron.

Taking advantage of his momentary vulnerability, I planted my shoulder into his chest, and with all the force I could muster sent all two hundred twenty-five pounds of him flying into the opposite snowbank. I grabbed a handful of snow before he could recover and dumped it on his stunned face. "And this is for decking me."

"Why you . . ." He struggled to his feet. I didn't stay around to hear the rest of his remark. Laughing, I sprinted straight through the middle of the fray and into the girls' dormitory. I didn't need to look over my shoulder to know that Kevin was close behind. Once inside the dormitory lobby, I made faces at the frustrated junior through the plate-glass window.

After a few minutes, I hurried to my room to change clothes. One glance at the clock reminded me that I had other classes besides first-period world history. Grabbing my books, I skated, slid, and jogged across campus to biology class. At the end of class, I hurried to the library to research information for my semester paper on the history of Greek theater during the life of Sophocles. I was immersed in Antigone's tragedies when I felt a tap on my shoulder. I looked around expecting to see Josh, but found Kevin's grinning face within inches of mine.

"You know, for a girl, you pack a pretty good wallop. You got me a good one."

"For a girl! How chauvinistic of you!"

He blushed. "Is this seat taken?"

"Uh . . ." I looked at my watch, then glanced around again for Josh. I'd expected him more than a half-hour ago. "No, help yourself. I'm just trying to decipher Sophocles. He makes no sense at all!"

Kevin tossed his stack of books on the table and sat down. "I know what you mean. Some of those Greek dudes are out to lunch. I mean, who cares whether or not Uncle Creon will let Antigone bury her brother Polynices?"

"Is that what all the hoopla is about?" Surprised, I studied Kevin's smirking face. I hadn't expected a "jock" to have heard of Sophocles, let alone understand his works.

Kevin yawned and opened the top book on his stack, a calculus book. "Yeah, it's just a tale of two hardheads going at it, both too proud to back down. Hey, is it true? You belong to Josh Hanson, don't you?"

"Excuse me?" I bristled. "For your information, I don't belong to anyone but myself. I am, however, dating Josh, if that's what you mean."

"Whatever."

"What do you mean, whatever?"

"Hey." He threw his hands defensively in the air. "It's not important, honest."

I stiffened my neck and glared at him through shaded eyes. "Well, it is to me. Slavery in this country went out nearly a hundred and fifty years ago, remember?"

A smile crinkled one side of his mouth. "Pretty independent, considering you're dating a theology major."

My left eyebrow disappeared into my hairline. "I beg your pardon?"

"Hey, I didn't make the rules."

"Rules? What rules?"

"That theology guys usually go for the simpering-type female. You know, the girls who will make good preachers' wives without overshadowing their husbands."

I growled underneath my breath, then smiled a ditsy smile and batted my eyelashes. "Oh, do you mean like you phys-ed men date blond cheerleader types because they look so adorable by your sides?"

For a second, Kevin worked a muscle in his left cheek, then broke into a grin. "Ya got me. Are we even now?"

I batted my lashes again. "Why, Mr. Bennett, whatever can you mean?" I simpered. "We Southern magnolias would never presume . . ."

"More like steel magnolia! Come off it," he whispered between a clenched-teeth smile. "I said I was sorry. Friends?" He held out his hand.

I smiled and took his proffered hand. "Friends, if you'll agree that you won't make assumptions about me and I won't about you."

"Agreed." He held my hand an instant too long.

I glanced down at my hand, then back at him. "My hand? I've grown rather fond of it over the years."

"And a mighty pretty hand it is." He lifted it to his lips.

I skillfully slipped it from his grasp. "My, my, Colonel Sanders, are you flirting with me?"

"Colonel Sanders! Kentucky Fried Chicken!" He ran his hand through his thick, dark brown hair. "If you have to ask, I must be out of practice. Sheesh! That's what I get for spending too much time working out in the gym!"

I laughed out loud. A young woman trying to study at the

next table shushed me. I giggled and buried my head in my stack of almost forgotten books.

"I hope I'm not out of line for asking this, but seriously, Heather, are you going with Josh Hanson?"

I thought for a moment. "I really don't know. Not formally, anyway."

Kevin's brown eyes darkened. "Well, everyone thinks you are, at least, everyone in Norton Hall. Josh has let it be known to the upper-division guys that you're definitely off-limits."

Off-limits? I wasn't sure how I felt about that. Did I really want to be off-limits? And did that put Josh off-limits with other girls?

Kevin leaned closer. He placed his right arm across the back of my chair and his left on the table in front of me. A teasing dimple deepened in his right cheek. "So are you? Off-limits, I mean?"

My pulse raced. *This is one guy who can give Josh Hanson a run for his money. And I thought I was ready to begin writing Mr. and Mrs. Hanson on my stationery?* I nibbled on my lower lip. My hands worried my tooth-scarred pen. "I-I-I'm not sure." Lifting my eyes to meet his, I added, "Can I, uh, get back to you on that?"

He leaned back in his chair and sent me a rakish grin that caused my heart to skip a beat. "You can count on it." Somehow I knew he meant what he said. "So, ya wanna grab a sandwich at the snack shop?"

"Sorry, but I have a lunch date with Josh, at least, I think I do." I glanced around the almost-empty library. "Maybe another time."

Kevin nodded, gathered his books together, and stood up. With his free hand he brushed a lock of renegade curls from the side of my face. "I'll be eagerly awaiting your answer."

As he walked toward the door, I took a deep breath and stared unseeing at the Third Ode of Antigone in an effort to regain my equilibrium. My thoughts tumbled around in my brain like a pair of tennies in the dorm clothes dryer. Josh, Kevin—Kevin, Josh. I shook my head and reread the ancient Greek passage. Some time later, my watch beeped twelve, and I hurried across campus to the cafeteria to meet Josh.

The instant I located him in the food line, I sensed trouble. His icy blue eyes turned me stone cold. The only other time I had seen him so angry was the day he lost a theological debate with one of his professors. When I questioned him, he denied being angry, only "righteously indignant."

I ignored his glare, picked up a tray, and joined him in line. "Hi, how was your morning? How'd you do on the Greek quiz?"

Josh stared down the length of his straight patrician nose at me, then turned to the food server. "I'll have a serving of mashed potatoes, gravy, and some of the roast, please." He slid his tray to the end of the line, poured himself a glass of grape juice, fixed himself a tossed salad, checked out at the cashier, and found an isolated table, all without saying one word to me.

I timidly followed, unsure of what he expected from me. By the time I reached the table, he'd said his own blessing and begun eating. Miffed, I placed my tray across the table from him instead of next to him. "Would you mind telling me what is wrong with you?"

I waited for him to pull out my chair. He didn't move. Resigned, I pulled out my own chair and sat down. "Did something terrible happen? Did you flunk the quiz?"

He plowed his fork into the mound of mashed potatoes.

I leaned forward, putting my face directly in his. "Josh? What is going on? Why are you acting like this?"

He lifted his head, and with the air of a barely tolerant monarch, he said, "Heather, the cafeteria is hardly the time or the place. We will talk about this later."

We will talk about this later? I shoved my chair back and leapt to my feet. "Fine! Enjoy your meal."

I whirled about and headed for the closest exit. I didn't realize Josh was behind me until we reached the foyer and he grabbed my arm. He whipped me about to face him. Shaking his finger in my face, he ordered, "Don't you ever embarrass me like that in public again. Do you understand?"

Instantly, my blood pressure skyrocketed to dangerous levels. "Excuse me? You were the rude and insensitive clod who didn't have enough manners to carry my tray or seat me at the table or at least wait until I was seated before wolfing down your food!" Pointing straight at his nose, I added, "So, don't you ever embarrass me like that in public again—do you understand?"

Fighting back tears, I wrenched my arm free of his grasp, grabbed my coat and books, and dashed from the building.

". . . Since I Found You"

JOSH

Mac! The woman drove me crazy. I thought about her day and night. I never could figure her out. One moment she was an artist, recreating the delicate beauty of a Chopin étude on the piano; the next, a little girl, giggling over some stupid joke or crying over a dead squirrel on the dormitory lawn. Then, right before my eyes, she'd metamorphose into a serious scholar with a rapier wit and an even sharper tongue. At the next glance, I'd discover an intriguing mystery woman, tempting me to lose myself in her copper brown eyes and her fiery red curls. I guess you could say I was smitten.

The more I got to know Heather, the more determined I became that she would one day become Mrs. Joshua Hanson. When her parents visited campus, I put on my best. Mrs. MacKenna seemed a bit aloof, but Mr. MacKenna and Heather's sister René welcomed me into their family circle.

I put on my most engaging smile and set out to win the woman's favor. *Mama,* I thought, *you might be reserved at first, but sooner or later, I'll win you over.* After all, if I possessed one talent, it was charm, especially with women. My mother said I began to flirt the moment the doctor first placed me in her arms. However, I knew I'd have to be careful and take it slow. But sooner or later, mama bear would be eating out of my hand.

Yes, slow *is the operative word here.* I definitely didn't want my relationship with Mac to end up like the last one, the one with Jennifer. My conscience still stung from that little, uh, summertime indiscretion. Knowing Mac meant more to me than Jen ever could, I waited three weeks before I even tried to kiss her. My schedule called for four weeks, but, well, what can I say? The woman literally threw herself at me.

It was in the fine-arts building. In order to spend extra time together, I took my Greek notes into the practice studio and studied while Mac practiced for her juries. I respected her determination to do well. For music-performance majors, juries are the final exam. They must perform three major pieces of music from memory. If someone messes up on his juries, he will have wasted an entire quarter and risked losing his music-major status.

To be honest, I'm not too sure I'd like standing alone in front of the entire theology faculty and reciting, from memory, three long Scripture passages in Greek, then defending my interpretation of the reading.

Anyway, one afternoon, when I arrived at the practice room, I opened the door a crack and, without warning, Mac leapt into my arms. She'd worked out some problem she'd been having in one of the pieces. Well, I guess I did what any red-blooded American male would do. I kissed her.

To say that the kiss shook me all the way to my red Nike swooshes would be an understatement. And from the way Mac held onto me, I knew she'd responded in kind. Jolted by the unexpected electricity between us, I gently pushed her away to the safety of arms' length. *And I wondered if there'd been any sexual chemistry between Jennifer and me?*

When I tried to speak, my voice was husky with emotion. "Mac." I looked down into her bewildered eyes. "I-I-I—"

"Oh, Josh, I'm sorry, I-I was so excited I couldn't wait—"

I titled her chin up until her lips were within an inch of mine and searched her eyes. "Are you really sorry, Mac?"

Her shoulder-length curls brushed against my hand as she shook her head gently. "I'm glad," I whispered. I dipped my head forward ever so slightly and kissed her again. The sound of approaching footsteps in the hall broke the magic of the moment. When Carl, my roommate, appeared in the doorway, Heather skittered across the room to the window.

"Hey, Josh, I'm scheduled to preach this weekend at a little church about twenty miles from here, but my folks want me to come home for some kind of family reunion. Can you cover for me?"

I cleared my raspy throat before answering. "Sure thing, buddy."

As theology majors at a small Christian college, we were expected to preach at the churches surrounding the college so many times each quarter. While Carl and I discussed the weekend arrangements, Mac studied some distant point in the parking lot behind the music building. Carl glanced over my shoulder at her.

"Heather, you sing, don't you? You did a great job at the Freshman Talent Night during Freshman Week. Would you be willing to either do a vocal or piano solo for special music for the church service?"

When Mac turned toward him, her face was still flushed. "Uh, I don't know . . ."

Carl grinned, then persisted with his sales job. "You know, I bet you two would sound great together. She's a fabulous alto, Josh. Her voice is as smooth as Christmas Eve fudge."

Mac blushed uncomfortably. I came to her rescue. "OK, Carl. One of us will cover special music for you too. But you owe me, man."

Carl thanked us both and left, pleased that his problem was solved. I closed the studio door and leaned against it. I wondered if I should bring up the subject of the kiss. "Mac?"

She took a deep breath, then turned to face me. "Any ideas on what we might be able to work up before the weekend? I have a couple gospel hymnbooks in my music locker."

As she brushed past me, I caught her arm. She paused. I slid my hand to her shoulder, placed my second hand on her other shoulder, and turned her to face me. "I didn't presume too much, did I, kissing you like that?"

She titled her head teasingly toward me, arched an eyebrow, and grinned. "Maybe a little—on the first kiss."

"And the second?"

"I'd better go get that music." She slipped from my hold and ducked out of the room into the hallway. Seconds later, she returned with a huge stack of songbooks, everything from country to classical to contemporary Christian.

Glancing through a book of country favorites, I found a hymn I'd sung many times in my home church in California. I showed it to her and suggested we start with something simple. She readily agreed. We tried singing one verse of "Precious Lord, Take My Hand" together and realized our voices blended perfectly, as if we'd been singing together for years.

We're going to make a great evangelistic team, I thought. We had such fun singing neither of us realized how much time had passed until my stomach announced a hunger attack. I looked at the clock on the wall and groaned. We'd missed supper at the cafeteria. I suggested we grab a sandwich and fries at College Town, the off-campus snack shop.

I helped Mac on with her ski jacket, adjusted her lavender woolen scarf about her neck, then kissed her again. This time she met me halfway.

As we left the music building and strolled along the main street of the little midwestern community, I held her close by my side. We grabbed a snack, then headed to the women's dorm. It was early, but she reminded me that she had a number of themes to finish for her freshman English class.

Before saying good night, I kissed her one more time. Her eyes sparkled with happiness as she bade me good night. She waved and skipped inside the dormitory. I watched until she disappeared from sight. *There's goes my future wife—no doubt about it.* I didn't need a mirror to know I was grinning like a Cheshire cat.

I strolled back to my dormitory, oblivious to the subzero temperatures. By the time I entered my dorm room, my euphoria became more reasonable. *I can't lose my head,* I told myself. I still need to proceed with caution. I lay down on my bed and recalled the kisses we'd shared. I remembered the willingness with which she melted into my arms. Suddenly doubts surfaced. *Is Mac really the woman of virtue she pretends to be?*

Over the next few days, I analyzed her every action. I didn't consciously put her to the test, but I did watch. She breezed through every situation, except one. Looking back, it was no big deal, really. Six years ago, however, it was a big deal.

At the time I didn't realize it, but I had this image of the perfect pastor's wife, a woman who would be the virtuous Mary, the mother of Jesus, in public and in my arms, in the privacy of our bedroom, I wanted a Mary Magdalene. Of course, I expected to marry a woman who saved herself for marriage. Considering my future career moves, I wouldn't consider buying used merchandise. The fact that I wouldn't be coming to her as pure never crossed my mind.

It was just before Christmas break; we'd been making out in the practice studio almost every afternoon since that first kiss. And, well, it got pretty hot. I have to admit I was disappointed when Mac didn't try to stop me sooner when I slid my hand under her blouse. And later, I couldn't help but wonder, *If we'd been up at Make-out Point instead of in the music building, would she have stopped me then? Maybe that playful innocence of hers isn't as genuine as it seems.* I had to be cautious.

During the days preceding Christmas break, it seemed Mac set out to purposely anger me. Whenever we were with our friends, she always seemed to be center stage, flaunting her beauty and her wit. *How unseemly*, I thought. *Why haven't I noticed this tendency in her before?*

I talked with my roommate about her. You see, Carl had a theory about preacher's wives. For obvious reasons, he and a number of my other theology-major friends refused to date women who were too attractive, too ambitious, or too bright. A pretty wife would tempt other men to lust after her. An ambitious wife would never agree to put her husband's ministry first. And an intellectual wife would always be challenging his authority. After our talk, I began to think that perhaps Carl's theory merited further study. Maybe Heather was just too pretty to be an effective pastor's wife—and too outspoken.

I continued to evaluate everything Heather said and did. I'd almost decided Carl's theory was wrong, when the day of the big snowstorm arrived. It was the first of the season. Without intending to, we left the cafeteria after breakfast and found ourselves in the middle of a snowball fight. In the process, we got separated. I chased my friend Brad halfway across campus after I took a direct hit to the side of the head. I evened the score with a full body tackle and face plant, then headed back to the cafeteria to find Mac. I found her, all right, wrestling in the snow with a dumb jock, and loving it! Furious that she'd play around with that Neanderthal, I stormed to my dorm room.

I tried to study, but all I could think about was the woman I planned to marry rolling on the ground in Kevin Bennett's arms. *Doesn't she have any decency? Any sense of proper decorum?* I paced my 10 x 10-foot dorm room. When my anger swelled to the point of wanting to smash my fist through the cement block wall, I decided it would be wiser and less painful to head to the gym for a workout. I almost hoped to run into Bennett. I fantasized about punching his lights out.

Fantasized was definitely the operative word. The man towered over my six-foot frame by at least four inches and outweighed me by a good forty pounds. The man could bench-press me and seven of my nearest and dearest friends, all at one time!

Bennett wasn't there. I changed into my swim trunks and did a mile and a half in the pool. By the time I showered and dried off, I'd cooled down to reason. As I combed my damp hair into place, I argued with myself in the mirror. My reflection and I came to the same logical conclusion. *It was a snowball fight, right? How much choice did Mac have being steamrolled by a Peterbilt semi?*

I'd told her at breakfast I'd meet her in the library and walk her to the cafeteria for lunch. I threw on my clothes and dashed across campus. As I entered the library, I met Mac's roommate Chris coming out of the building.

"Hi, have you seen Mac? She asked me to meet her . . ." I couldn't miss the strange look on Chris's face. "Is something wrong? Where is she?"

Chris pointed toward the upstairs window and stammered

nervously, "She's in the liberal arts room."

"Thanks." Before I could ask what was wrong, Chris was halfway to the administration building. I took the stairs, two at a time, and rushed into the study room. Ten feet, and I screeched to a halt. Sitting at a table across the room, with her back to me, I saw Heather. Kevin sat on the chair next to her, leaning over her, his arm around her shoulder. I considered charging like a wounded bull until I heard her flirty laugh. I stopped, whirled about, and thundered down the stairs and out of the building. I rushed back to my dorm room. My roommate Carl glanced up from his Greek notes. "Hey, do you remember the conjugation for *trust*?"

I ripped my carefully devised schedule from my bulletin board and tore it to shreds. "This is what I think of trust!" I shouted. He watched as I threw the paper into the trash and bolted from the room.

I reached the cafeteria seconds before Mac arrived. I'd just picked up my meal tray when she entered the dining hall. I looked around for Kevin, but he was nowhere in sight. *Coward!* I grumbled. When she saw me, she waved and smiled, which made me all the angrier. So angry, in fact, that if I'd spoken to her I would have said something I wasn't sure I was ready to say. I maintained my cool reserve until we reached the table. Instead of sitting next to me, she chose a confrontational position across from me.

As she pulled out her own chair, I glanced up at her. The hurt I saw in her eyes infuriated me all the more. *How dare you act like the injured party here! How dare you try to make me feel like the heel!* I jammed my fork into my mashed potatoes and shoveled it into my mouth.

She asked me what was wrong. Knowing I would lose what cool I had managed to maintain, I suggested we talk about it later, in private. For some reason, my suggestion teed her off. She jumped up from the table, shouted something about enjoying my meal, and ran from the dining room. As I pushed back my chair and stood up, I could feel a hundred eyes staring at me. I'd never been so mortified by a woman in my life. I rushed after her, stopping her by the cafeteria's outside doors. If our relationship was to last, she needed to know that I would not tolerate being made a fool of in public. And I told her so. Instead of showing remorse or humility, she threw my admonition right back in my face. Infuriated, I clenched and unclenched my fists as I watched her run toward the women's dormitory.

After wasting the afternoon in classroom lectures I didn't even hear, I grabbed my jacket from the coat rack and stormed out into the night. As I half-walked, half-jogged on the icy sidewalk, I couldn't erase the picture of Kevin Bennett and Mac from my mind. *How dare she be angry with me! I'm the injured party here. How can she be so unreasonable?*

I trudged on past the edge of town, where the sidewalks stopped and the country road began. The town faded from my view. I pounded out my frustration with each step. "Why, God, why?" I shouted into the crystal-clear night. "I'm training to serve You. Look at all I've given up for You. I believed You brought Heather and me together. Now, I'm not so sure!"

I stopped in the middle of the road and shook my fists in God's face. "Come on, tell me! Say something! I'm doing this for You!"

No voice called to me out of the darkness. Only the sound of the arctic breeze whipping about my face. I broke into a run. In time, I outran my anger. I paused to catch my breath. I could see a few points of light from farmhouses and the silhouettes of trees and silos against the horizon on all sides. The sky had cleared. Stars shone like a million diamond chips tossed on a swatch of black velvet. I gazed at the darkened prairie and pretended I viewed the Pacific Ocean from my bedroom window at our home south of Crescent City, California. And except for the sight of my breath each time I exhaled, it worked.

I couldn't believe it; I was homesick for the first time in my life. I thought about my mom. I trusted her wisdom. If anyone knew about life, she did. Her bravery had seen her through the tough days after my father walked out on us, through a marriage to an abusive alcoholic, a second divorce, the trials of raising a son alone and going back to school nights to get her college degree and master's in counseling. I could almost hear her voice telling me to go back to Mac and work it out. "Remember, Josh, there are always two sides of a story."

"Not this time, Mom," I shouted into the darkness. "I mean, the guy was all over her." Silence followed. *First God, then my mother!* I trudged farther until the cold seeped through my boots to my toes. My nose and ears felt as if they'd break off. I turned around and headed back to town. *All right, everyone's entitled to one mistake. I'll give her a chance to apologize. I'll forgive her for her indiscretion. But it had better never happen again!*

Chapter Three:

"Wounded Hearts . . ."

HEATHER

Angry? Mad? I was furious! I had no idea what had gotten into Josh. He was being totally unreasonable. I burst through the main doors of the women's dormitory into the lobby and ran headlong into Kevin.

"Hey, what's wrong? Are you all right?"

"What are you doing here?" I demanded.

Startled, he answered, "I was dropping off a copy of—hey, why am I telling you this?"

I swiped at a tear sliding down my cheek.

"Hey, what's wrong?" He tilted my chin upward and searched my face for answers. All I could do was shake my head and gulp back my tears. "What happened? Is it your folks? Josh?"

I nodded. Kevin led me to an empty sofa.

"Which is it? Your folks or Josh?"

I shook my head and nodded.

"Josh? Josh did something to you? What? What did he do?"

I sniffed. Kevin walked to the main desk and returned with a handful of tissues. He handed them to me. I blew my nose. "I'm sorry, Kevin. Thank you for being so nice, but I've got to work this out alone."

I ran up the stairs to my room and threw myself onto my bed. I was thankful Chris wasn't in the room. I didn't feel like talking to anyone. Burying my face in my pillow, I sobbed out my frustrations. As nice as Kevin might be, I really cared for

Josh, maybe even loved him.

Maybe Josh and I are spending too much time together, I thought. *Maybe we need a cooling-off period.* Even as I considered being apart from Josh, my heart rejected the idea. During the last few weeks, I'd fashioned my entire life around him. Every waking moment, I either thought about him or was with him.

I remembered the advice my mother gave before I left for college. "Find yourself and who you are before you settle for one man. Remember, God's plan for your life will make you the happiest." It sounded so wise when she said it, but at this point in my life, highly impractical.

I glanced at the Bible I kept on the stand beside my bed. I picked it up and tried to read. Somehow Jonah and his troubles didn't hold my attention. I returned the Bible to the stand. My conscience reminded me that I should go practice the piano. Instead, I wrapped myself in the afghan my grandmother made for my high-school graduation and snuggled down to sleep. The telephone jangled me awake. I picked up the receiver and identified myself.

"You have a guest in the lobby," the dormitory receptionist said.

I rubbed the sleep from my eyes. "Who is it?"

"Josh Hanson." She didn't hesitate. Every woman on campus knew Josh Hanson. I glanced at the clock. *Where had the evening gone?*

"Tell him to go away. I don't want to see him." Blindly I grabbed a tissue from the box beside my bed and blew my nose. My head throbbed with pain. I hated it when I cried.

"He says to beg you to come downstairs to talk with him."

I sighed in the darkness. *I must look a mess.* I turned on my desk lamp and peered into the wall mirror. My eyes were bloodshot and puffy. Red blotches covered my face.

The voice on the other end of the phone called, "What shall I tell him?"

"Tell him I'll be down in five minutes." I slammed down the receiver, ran to the sink, and splashed cold water on my face. A dab of coverup here, a swatch of blush and eye shadow there, and I realized I looked about as good as any redhead could look after a major bout of tears.

I didn't see Josh when I first entered the lobby. He sat with his back to me on a sofa over to one side of the parlor. He was reading a magazine and didn't see me coming. I paused behind the couch.

"Hi."

Josh leapt to his feet. "Oh, hi." He tossed the magazine down on the coffee table. "I'm glad you decided to come down and talk with me."

A group of my friends walked by the open French doors and waved. I waved back. He shifted his weight from one foot to the other. "Ya wanna go somewhere and talk? I've got my car outside."

I nodded. "I, uh, better get my jacket."

He nodded. "I'll wait right here."

"OK, I'll, uh, just go, uh, upstairs . . ." I backed out of the parlor, whirled about, and bounded up the stairs to my room. I caught a glimpse of my grinning face in the mirror. *Maybe everything's going to be all right after all.* I grabbed my ski jacket and returned to the parlor. He helped me on with my coat, zipping it up to the collar. After planting a kiss on the tip of my nose, he wrapped his arm about my waist and led me to his car.

The midnight-blue Grand Am, Josh's pride and joy, leapt to life with the turn of the key in the ignition. A hot jazz saxophone blared from the radio. He scanned the FM frequency until he found a soft jazz station. Natalie Cole's maple-syrup voice filled the car's interior. Josh glanced over at me. "Where to?"

I adjusted the seat belt across my lap. "Anywhere, just so we can talk."

He shifted the car into drive and nosed into the light evening traffic. Neither of us spoke for some time. I leaned back against the headrest, closed my eyes, and let the music wash over me. I wasn't any too eager to break the temporary peace treaty by getting into the cause of our disagreement.

I opened my eyes when I heard gravel replace the smooth

rhythm of the pavement. I recognized the spot immediately. Make-out Point. I'd never been there, but I'd heard about it from my friends. I could only see the silhouettes of two other cars at the far end of the parking area. I was about to object, when I spotted the dazzle of the town lights spread out below us. I gasped in surprise.

"Ya wanna get out of the car? You get a better view," he said.

I undid my seat belt and opened my door. I climbed out and walked to the point. Josh was right. With the stars above us and the lights of the town at our feet, we were surrounded by a magical midwinter light show. Josh came up behind me and slipped his arms about my waist. I leaned my head back against his chest. He nibbled my left ear. His warm breath sent chills down my spine. I felt my insides pleasantly contract.

"It's so beautiful," I whispered.

"Yes, you are." I felt, rather than heard, his reply. For one minute I was staring at the lights and the next, he'd spun me about in his arms and we were kissing, spinning out of control on a whirling carousel. Lightheaded with passion, I couldn't think. I knew I should be angry with him, but I couldn't remember why. Happily, I abandoned myself to his kisses. Before long, the subzero temperatures sent us scurrying back to the warmth of the Grand Am.

I hopped into the car and shivered. "It sure is cold out there tonight."

Josh climbed in his side, shut the door, and started the engine. Instantly, the music from the radio resumed as waves of warm air swept through the car. He reached up and opened the sunroof. "We can still watch the stars together."

I eyed him apprehensively. "Isn't it dangerous to sit in a car with the engine running? Carbon-monoxide poisoning or something?"

He laughed. "Not with the sunroof open." He lowered his seat to a full reclining position. "Ah, this is more like it. Pull that lever on the side of your seat."

I obeyed. The seat lowered me into his waiting arms. He

held me close as we watched the stars directly over our heads for some time. It was like being in our very own planetarium. I felt lazy and warm and loved. As he pointed toward Orion, his breath rustled the tiny curls along the side of my face. "See, there's one arm. There's the other. His two legs. Can you make out the sword hanging from his belt?"

I tried to make out the form of the mighty hunter.

"Some people say that's the area through which Jesus will return."

"Really?" I turned my face toward him. He looked at me at the same instant. He nodded his head slowly.

"That's what they say . . ." His words drifted off as we stared into each other's eyes. My interest in swords and hunters and constellations faded. I can't deny it, even after all that had happened between us, I wanted him to kiss me. He read my thoughts and obliged.

As the interior of the car heated up, he removed his jacket and tossed it into the back seat. Slowly, he unzipped my jacket and eased it off my shoulders and arms. When I shivered, he drew me closer. I melted into his embrace. I started when his hand slid beneath my sweater.

"Sh, darling," he whispered in my ear, nibbling on my ear lobe. "Relax, honey, I won't hurt you. Just relax."

I knew I should stop him, but the hand massaging my back felt so good. I allowed it to soothe away my worries. He kissed my neck, then rained a trail of kisses up to my lips. Lost in the magic of a deep kiss, I suddenly felt my bra unhook. I tensed. He held me against his chest and murmured in my ear. "Oh, Mac, you feel so good. It feels so right having you back in my arms."

My conscience fired the first shots of what would quickly become a major battle against the enemy within—myself. Searching for the courage to resist, I turned my head to one side. He continued massaging my upper back while his relentless barrage of kisses on my neck massaged away my misgivings. In one smooth motion, he leaned me back against my seat once more and slid his hand out from under me and onto my bare stomach. I'd gotten used to the feeling of his warm touch on my skin. And while I loathed stopping him, my senses told me I must. And soon! I knew I had to stop him soon.

Goose bumps sprang up on my rib cage as he lifted my sweater and buried his face in my stomach. I melted under the shower of kisses he rained across my stomach. When his hand advanced north, my reason returned. "Josh, I've never . . ."

He paused. I looked pleadingly into his deep blue eyes. "Oh, Josh, I don't think . . ."

"Don't think," he murmured, stifling my objections with a deep, passionate kiss and the rapid exploration of my upper body. I groaned when he removed his hand for an instant. Then suddenly he was back, pulling me to him, flesh against flesh. I'd never experienced such feelings, such emotion. No one had ever ignited my passion like this. I'd never felt so warm, so secure, yet so alive. He unzipped my jeans and slid his hand around my waist and down my back.

I ached to abandon all propriety, but the warning bells imbedded in the recesses of my mind clanged louder than ever. My words came in short, breathless gasps. "Josh, no . . . I can't . . . I just can't. Please . . . please . . . I don't want to . . . we've got to stop." I placed my hands in the center of his bare chest and pushed halfheartedly against him.

"Heather, it's OK." He grabbed my hands and wrapped them around his neck. I could see the sweat glistening on his bare chest and on his forehead. "Come on, you can't stop now. It would be inhuman to stop me now. You know you want it just as much as I do."

I struggled out of his grasp. "No! Not like this, I don't!"

I felt as well as heard the growl from deep in his chest as he let go of me and fell back against his seat. "You can't do this to me, Mac. I'm a man. I have needs."

Before I could change my mind, I popped the seat lever. My seat flew forward. With unsteady hands, I reached for the seat belt. "So do I, just not now, not yet." I wrestled to straighten my garments. "When the right times comes, it will be different."

He ran his fingers through his hair, then pounded the steering wheel with his fists. "You're just like the others, Mac, a tease. When it comes to putting out, you chicken out."

What an insult! Can't he see I'm not teasing? While I couldn't understand how uncomfortable a guy felt when his libido was doused with ice water, I now knew, for the first time, how frustrated a woman felt in a similar condition. I took a deep, ragged breath. "I'm sorry, Josh, but you must know I wasn't teasing. I just couldn't go any farther, not here like this. It would be wrong."

"Don't crawl behind the religion thing with me. Remember, if you wanted it, you already committed adultery in your mind, remember?"

"I don't think that is what—"

"Oh, just, just leave me alone. I'm too frustrated to talk right now." He again pounded his fist against the steering wheel, denting it.

He silently stared out the side window and rubbed his bruised fist while I huddled miserably in my seat. Five minutes passed. Finally, I said, "I think you'd better take me back to the dorm now."

Without a word, he closed the sunroof. Then, "You're right. I think I'd better take the little girl back to her dormitory and find myself a real woman." He jammed the gears into reverse, shifted to drive, and spun out, spewing gravel for a fifteen-foot radius.

He couldn't have hurt me more than if he'd slapped me across the face. We rode in silence like strangers. The car screeched to a stop in front of my dorm. Josh's arm brushed purposely across my chest as he opened my door. I pushed him away and opened the door myself. "Josh, don't. Don't ruin everything we have."

"Just what did we have? A few kisses, a laugh or two, a squeeze?" he hissed.

I touched the side of his tightened jaw. "I'm sorry, I don't know what to say."

He stared straight ahead. "Say goodbye."

"Is that it, then—goodbye, for us, I mean? Are you saying that if I won't put out, you walk?" Bitter anger, like bile, bubbled up inside my throat. I swung my feet out of the car into the slushy gutter. "If that's the way it is between us, you're right. Maybe it's for the best. Goodbye, Josh; have a great life."

I stood, straightened my shoulders, and sloshed through the melting snow toward the dormitory, determined to keep my head high and my dignity intact. Once I reached my room, I fell apart into a heap on my bed. My roommate Chris abandoned her calculus book and ran to my side.

"Heather? What's the matter, kiddo?"

Clutching my pillow to my chest, I curled into a fetal ball. "Josh and I broke up," I stammered. "This time, for good."

"What happened?"

I shook my head. While a part of me wanted to tell her everything, another part of me hesitated to speak, refusing to believe it was really over for us. She rubbed my back while I sobbed into my pillow. When I finally regained control, I took a long shower. As the hot, steamy spray washed away my tears, I considered calling home. I longed to hear my mother's voice, to hear her say it was all right, that I'd be fine. But I knew that if I did call her, she'd want to know all the details. I couldn't tell her how I'd wanted to go all the way as much as Josh. How could she understand the passion of the moment? So many times I'd heard the story of their courtship. Daddy, the perfect gentleman, and Mama having never even kissed a boy before he entered her life.

I needed to talk with someone, but whom? My friends wouldn't understand. While Chris didn't sleep around, she did "put out" if she really liked the guy. And Andrea, in the room next door, well, she bragged about her conquests. She'd only laugh at my guilt over the petting Josh and I had done. Her roommate Rhea, poor little Rhea, had never even dated a guy, let alone made out with him.

I let the biting hot shower spray pummel my neck and back. Something had changed inside me. Feelings had been awakened that terrified me. I'd never been so close to losing control in my entire life. For that matter, I'd often laughed when girls talked about going so far that they didn't want to stop, that they knew they were making a terrible mistake, but went ahead anyway. I could now understand. It had taken all my strength to remove Josh's hands from my body, to break the bond of electrifying warmth and eager anticipation for the unknown.

For the first time I understood why my Christian teachers advised waiting until one's wedding night to awaken one's natural sexual hunger. Even in the safety of the shower, I couldn't dislodge the curious temptation to imagine what it would have been like if I hadn't resisted.

". . . and Broken Dreams"

JOSH

I don't think I'd ever been so frustrated or so angry in my life as I was the night Mac and I broke up. So much for trying to give Mac room to apologize for her childish exit from the cafeteria! And she still hadn't explained why I'd seen her in another man's arms twice in one day.

The only thing that kept me from putting my fist through a mirror or something was my healthy fear of pain. Instead of breaking something, I took a cold shower. Some authorities say that when it comes to cooling sexual desires, there's nothing to the cold-shower myth. That night, I believed they might be right.

I'll admit we went at it pretty heavy out there at Make-out Point that night. I think the windows would have steamed over even on an August afternoon from the heat we managed to generate. I honestly didn't go out there to score. I knew we'd probably mess around some, but I never dreamed she'd allow any heavy petting. Maybe if I'd taken it a little slower . . .

Actually, if the truth be told, a part of me was relieved when Mac insisted on stopping. Yet I couldn't help but wonder how many other guys she'd allowed to paw her body before putting on the brakes. My anger surfaced again. *No,* I reminded myself, *that's not fair. She did stop me.*

I decided she'd passed a test. Not with an A+, like I'd hoped my future wife would, but at least a C+ or a B-. On the ride home, I had expected her to apologize for allowing me to go as far as we did. That would have upped her grade a little. I believed confession was good for the soul.

You may wonder how I could condemn Mac for being a willing participant and not condemn myself as well. I've wondered the same thing many times since. All I can say is, like many of my friends, I rationalized away whatever responsibility I might feel with the old adage, "It's up to the girl to put on the brakes," preferably before things get too hot. I honestly believed I had the right to expect a good girl to put on the brakes, if she, indeed, was a good girl. And if she wasn't, hey, she was the one who seduced me, right? So why should I feel guilty? After all, "Boys will be boys," right?

Still frustrated, I glanced at my desk clock and realized the gym would be open for at least another hour. I decided to shoot a few hoops with the guys and forget women existed. It worked on the court, but the minute I went to shower, my humiliation returned. By the time I dressed, I'd conjured up a massive pity party. Instead of heading back to the dormitory, I walked down a familiar side street, the street in front of Jennifer Renfro's apartment. Filled with self-pity, I stood outside her building, looking at the light shining through her bedroom window. By the time I rang her doorbell, I'd placed the blame for the night's fiasco, past, present, and whatever the future might bring, squarely on Heather's shoulders. She'd tempted me beyond what I could bear. Even God didn't do that, I reasoned.

Jen welcomed me with open arms. Here was a woman who appreciated me. Thinking of that night six years down the road, I can't decide if I turned to Jen for comfort or for self-punishment. After all, guilt is guilt. I reasoned that if the Bible says lusting after a woman is the same as committing adultery, why not go all the way and enjoy the pleasure of the sin. And with Jennifer, there were all kinds of pleasure.

I left the apartment just before dawn. As I stumbled through the darkness toward the men's dormitory, my mouth tasted bitter. I could smell Jen's perfume on my body. Already, I regretted the series of hasty decisions I'd made. Again, I blamed Jen for seducing me. After all, I just turned to her for a little conversation, a little comfort. Then I remembered Mac.

My head pounded from lack of sleep. I felt grimy and smelly. I took a quick shower, then rehearsed my apology to Mac in front of my shaving mirror. After I finished dressing, I rushed to the cafeteria. Mac sat at a table eating breakfast with her roommate.

What luck, I thought and sat my tray down next to Heather's. "Is this seat taken?"

Color rose to Heather's cheeks. Before she could answer, Kevin Bennett and two of his jock buddies stepped up to the table. Kevin edged his tray between Mac and me. "Sorry, sport, but I'm sitting here."

I glared at Mac. "Didn't waste any time, did you?" She dropped her head. I walked to an empty table on the opposite side of the cafeteria.

The next two months were miserable. Everywhere I went, I saw Kevin and Mac together. It's not as if I could have avoided her. Since we first sang together, she and I had become a popular musical duo on campus. Even after breaking up, we were regularly asked to sing together for banquets, parties, church, and other religious services. After talking it over, we agreed to behave like adults. However, whenever we practiced or performed, Kevin always managed to be there, sitting on the sidelines, applauding our efforts.

I think I dated a different girl every weekend throughout the winter quarter. I figured that my carefully planned life schedule was out the window anyway, but maybe, with a little luck, I could meet another Mac and get it back on track. However, I didn't want another Mac. I wanted Mac!

One afternoon, the week before Valentine's, I found her alone in the practice studio. When I grinned and waved from the doorway, she asked if I'd come to practice the number we were scheduled to sing for the college faculty's Valentine's banquet.

I glanced around the doorjamb. The folding chair was empty—no Kevin. I couldn't suppress the grin that leapt to my face. "No, but since I'm here, we might as well."

She took out a piece of sheet music and placed it on the piano. "Dean Willows asked if we'd do this song. It's his and his wife's twentieth anniversary."

I read the title aloud—"Can't Help Falling in Love With You." "Ah, an old Elvis Presley hit. Sure, let's try it." Apologies to the "king of pop," but the song was made for our voices. When Vanessa Jakes, a junior piano-performance major, drifted by the practice studio, Mac asked her if she would accompany us.

We sang the words to one another, Mac on one side of the piano bench and me on the other. Electricity flowed between us. Tears misted in her eyes. To diffuse my emotions, I winked and blew her a kiss.

After going through the number twice, Vanessa announced she was late for an appointment with her major professor and left. Mac and I looked at one another uncomfortably. We hadn't been alone since the night at the point. Mac gathered her music books in her arms. "Uh, I guess we'd better be going."

I walked her to her music locker and lingered as she placed the books on her locker shelves. "Kevin picking you up for supper?"

She shook her head. Her coppery brown eyes lacked their usual luster. "He's over at the gym. He has a big game tonight."

"Any place you're supposed to be?"

Again, she shook her head. "How about you?"

"Nowhere but here." I helped her into her coat. "Mac, do you think we could go somewhere and talk? Maybe over to College Town?"

"I'd like that." She grinned sheepishly. "But I don't think Kevin would."

"We'll go Dutch; then it won't be a date. Will that help?"

She laughed. "I guess."

As we sipped two old-fashioned chocolate ice-cream sodas, Mac talked for the first time about the day we broke up. I confessed my jealousy at seeing her with Kevin. She explained what had actually happened that day in the library.

For all our honesty with one another, we avoided mentioning the encounter at Make-out Point. Maybe if we had, maybe we could have avoided the mistakes of the future.

After our talk at College Town, we found it easier to be friends again, which only reminded me of what I'd lost. In March, Mac and I were invited to do a twenty-minute concert at a major Collegiates for Christ youth congress in a town thirty miles or so from campus. Vanessa Jakes, our accompanist, would be along, as well as the school's fifteen-member gymnastics team and their coach. I decided to drive my Grand Am rather than ride the touring bus. Vanessa begged to ride with me, since riding a school bus made her nauseated. That's when I learned that Kevin would be at our afternoon concert.

The music and the preaching at the youth congress were fantastic. With so many kids crowded into the convention center, I didn't see much of either Mac or Vanessa until our dress rehearsal, two hours before the concert. Vanessa arrived backstage about the same time as I, but not alone. She introduced me to Ben Abbott, a third-year medical student, attending a nearby medical school. He excused himself and took a seat out front of the curtain. Vanessa continued to glow.

"We met during the seminar on mission outreach this morning. When Ben finishes his residency, he plans to enlist for mission service. Isn't that exciting?" I'd never seen Vanessa so wired. I envied her. "His parents are stationed on Guam, you know, in the Pacific?"

I raised one eyebrow. "I do know where Guam is located."

She giggled and blushed. "I'm sorry. Hey, you wouldn't be offended if I didn't ride with you tonight, would you? Ben's offered to take me back to campus."

"Hmm, sounds serious."

Vanessa shrugged and grinned.

"Go ahead. Have fun, but don't do anything I wouldn't do."

"Tsk! Josh, I just met the guy, remember?" She walked over to the piano and began our opening number.

A few minutes later, Mac arrived. I knew instantly she'd been crying. Hope sprang up within me when I noticed Kevin was nowhere to be seen. I walked over to her.

"Hey, kid, what's wrong?"

She just shook her head. "Can we get this rehearsal over? I need to go and take a couple of aspirin before the concert. I have a splitting headache."

I smiled to myself as I obliged her by opening the curtains. My smile faded when I saw the frowning Kevin sitting in the front row beside Vanessa's doctor-to-be. I motioned to the sound man in the booth at the back of the auditorium. "Can we get a couple of hot mikes down here, please?"

Rehearsal was ragged. Heather kept forgetting the lyrics. If there'd been a way of canceling, I would have. To make it worse, the sound man and the lighting man kept messing up the taped introduction number and the place where Vanessa was to begin playing the live accompaniment. After five or six times through the program, I realized things weren't getting any better. I suggested we call it quits and meet again backstage fifteen minutes before the concert.

All participants readily agreed. I asked the audiovisual team to stay behind so we could iron out a few of the problems. Vanessa disappeared with Ben. Kevin and Mac left together, obviously resuming whatever discussion they'd been having before they arrived at the concert hall.

When I arrived for the concert, I found Mac backstage, sitting in the dark. I hurried to her. "Hey, kiddo, are you all right?"

She nodded and swiped away tears.

"Is there anything I can do?"

"No." She shook her head for emphasis.

I tilted her chin so that her eyes met mine. She didn't pull away. "I'm here for you if you need me." I had the worst urge to kiss her, but I knew better.

"Thanks . . ." Her voice drifted off. Behind us a door opened. A shaft of light fell across the floor to where we stood. I turned in time to see the door close again, then burst open. Vanessa bounded up the stairs.

"Hey, what's going on in here? Where's the light switch?" She flipped on the backstage light and looked at Mac. "Did you know Kevin is out in the hall looking for you?"

Mac sighed, then checked the cuffs on her suit jacket. "Well, I don't have time to deal with him right now."

The concert went well. I believe the Holy Spirit made up for the distractions. Heather's professionalism definitely overshadowed her emotions. To anyone other than me, she appeared happy and composed. After the concert, a number of people cornered me, requesting bookings at their churches. Before I could break free, Mac and Kevin had left the auditorium.

I drove back to campus that night. On my way into the dorm, I bounded up the stairs, straight into Kevin. He held two boxes of books in his arms. "Hey, man, what's up?"

"Headin' home for a quarter. Money's run out." He shifted the load of books in his arms.

"Sorry, man."

He snorted, then sneered at me. "Heather's all yours, Hanson. I've gotten everything out of her I want anyway. She's quite the hot little number, huh?"

I screeched to a halt, my hand frozen on the hall door's brass handle. "Excuse me? I don't know what you're talking about."

He smirked. "Oh, come on now, you dated Mac long enough to get a piece of the action. That little skirt can really put out. Or was she too much woman for you?"

I clenched and unclenched my fists. I wanted to sock his smirking mouth into the middle of next week. But I knew that if I hit him, I'd be the one traveling through time.

"Bennett, get out of my face, will ya?" I hauled the door open with the force of a hurricane. It slammed against the wall, just missing my knuckles by a millisecond.

Not waiting around for him to reply, I stormed down the hallway to my room. I couldn't remember ever being so angry. Visions of that Neanderthal clutching at, pawing Mac nauseated me. *How could you, Mac? How could you let that creep touch you?*

By the next morning, when I ran into Mac at the music building, I'd decided to forgive her. After all, women are the weaker sex. And I could see how some women might find

Kevin Bennett somewhat attractive. Yet my heart ached. As I watched her seated at the piano playing a difficult Mozart number, I silently pleaded, *"Why you, Mac?"*

When I entered the practice studio, she stopped playing and looked up at me. "Sorry to hear about Kevin," I began. *No, I'm not. Why did I say that?*

She smiled sadly. "It's OK. Of course I'm sorry he had to leave school, but it was pretty much over between us anyway. So, how do you think the concert went last night?"

"Great. Of course, I think we could do better if we practiced more." I measured my words and the tone of my voice carefully. "Oh, by the way, some guy connected with Gospel Records gave me his card and suggested we send him a demo. What do you think?"

She leapt from the bench. Hopping up and down while tugging on my jacket sleeves, she squealed, "You're kidding! Gospel Records? The biggest producer of contemporary Christian music?!"

I laughed. "Hey, watch the denim, kiddo. We haven't made a demo tape yet, let alone cut an album."

"But we will, right? We will. Have you told Vanessa the news?"

"Not yet. I haven't seen her this morning."

"Well, come on." She dragged me into the hallway. "She's practicing in studio five."

Vanessa's excitement over the possible demo matched Mac's. After discussing which of our songs we'd record, we set up a practice schedule.

When Vanessa left for her music theory class, I walked Mac to her dormitory. As we rounded the end of the building, I paused and turned to face her. "Do you think there's any chance we could possibly get back together now, with Kevin out of the picture?"

Mac glanced down at the slushy sidewalk, then up at me. "I, uh, don't know, Josh. I'm kind of bummed out on men right now. Give me time, and we'll see."

It wasn't the answer I wanted or even expected. I had to seize the moment. "We'd take it slower this time, honest."

She cast a sharp gaze toward the storm clouds overhead and bit her lower lip. Tears glistened in her eyes. "I don't know. I just don't know."

"OK, no promises about the future, right? I can handle that. How about just two friends meeting for supper tonight; then we can go directly to the fine-arts building to practice with Vanessa?"

She laughed and shook her head. "Josh, you are incorrigible. You're going to make a great preacher someday, or a snake-oil salesman."

Horrified, I sputtered, unable to come up with an appropriate reply. She placed a hand on my forearm. "Don't worry. I meant it as a compliment."

Chapter Four:

"Back Where
I Started . . ."

HEATHER

I guess I dated Kevin Bennett to spite Josh. I'm not very proud of that fact, but I'm afraid it's true. Once Kevin and I had discussed the Greek tragedies and a little Shakespeare, we had nothing left in common. As a physical education major, his life circled around sports. As a musician, I slept and ate Chopin, Bartók, and Liszt.

Most evenings after supper, I sat in the bleachers while he played ball—football, basketball, soccer. You name the game, and I sat through it. I'd hate to think how many winter quarter's Writing 101 compositions I wrote to the dribble of a basketball or punctuated to the blast from a referee's whistle.

However, it wasn't his on-the-court moves that bothered me the most, but the plays he attempted in his Jeep Cherokee. Stinging from Josh's accusations of being a tease, I probably gave away too much too soon. In fact, I know I did. While I refused to let him push me as far as Josh had gone, my bruised ego welcomed Kevin's tender ministrations sooner than was wise. With Kevin's size, I felt protected when I was with him. I liked that for a while until I discovered under the macho image was a spoiled little boy who threw tantrums whenever his ego was bruised.

Because Josh and I had often sung together while we were dating, we were still asked to perform at the college and in churches in the surrounding area. Our big break came when the music committee organizing the statewide Collegiates for Christ youth rally asked us to put together a twenty-minute sacred concert. The week before Josh and I performed our mini concert, I had already decided Kevin's and my relationship wasn't going anywhere and we needed to break it off. So when Kevin told me on the way to the rally that he would be leaving school for the rest of the winter quarter, I felt only relief.

Kevin had other ideas. He wanted me to promise not to date while he was gone. He'd never been happy having me sing with Josh in the first place. When I told him I thought it would be wiser for us both to date others during the interim, we began a battle that lasted throughout the weekend. Even the triumph of the concert didn't lessen the tension between Kevin and me.

By the time he dropped me off at my dormitory on Saturday night, we'd said all there was to say. Kevin demonstrated his fury by laying rubber away from the curb. I returned to my room, the happiest I'd felt in months. I made a vow to date around a while, to put in more time at the keyboard and with my Bible. I'd allowed my personal connection with Jesus to grow lukewarm since coming to college. I decided it was time to get back in tune with God.

That's why, the next day, when Josh asked me if we could begin dating again, I refused. I'd allowed both guys to chip away at my self-confidence, and I needed time to heal, to laugh, to be me. However, Josh persisted.

Ah, the value of hindsight. I look back now, from a six-year vantage point, and wish I'd resisted. Maybe if I'd been stronger, wiser . . . *Here I go again, second-guessing the past. Leave the past in the past, Heather!*

Josh won. We began dating less than a week after Kevin's departure—by default. We spent so much time together rehearsing for our demo tape, it was only natural to pick up our relationship from where we had stopped.

By the time Kevin returned to campus after spring break, Josh's and my relationship was firmly established. I did notice that Josh became quite protective of me whenever

Kevin was around. The biggest change in our relationship was due to Josh's new off-campus apartment. There, we could practice our music until all hours of the night without bothering or being bothered by anyone, since the couple living in the other half of the duplex were seldom home. Vanessa, our accompanist and backup singer, helped maintain the proper decorum for our jam sessions.

I especially enjoyed the weekends her boyfriend Ben, a third-year medical student from the university, visited for the weekend. We women would cook a special meal for our men, then spend the evening together, curled up on the oversized sofa watching videos, discussing politics, or listening to classical music.

Then there were the other times—times when things got too cozy between Josh and me, and I would put on the brakes. He would pout for hours. Whenever I tried to talk with him about these mood swings, he would apologize or say it was all my imagination. I didn't appreciate being made to feel guilty for doing the right thing.

One evening, we were alone in the apartment. His hand strayed to a particularly sensitive part of my anatomy. When I removed it and threatened to leave the apartment, I guess he thought I was leaving the relationship. He went into a rage. He grabbed my right arm and whirled me about.

I struggled. "Josh, let me go."

Wrenching my arm up behind my back, he growled into my ear. "No, you're mine. I'll never let you go."

Tears sprang into my eyes. I struggled. "Stop it! You're hurting me!"

After giving my arm one last tug, he let go. I carried the bruises for weeks. Now I realize I should have called it quits right then and there. *Oh, dear God, I'm doing it again—second-guessing myself.*

That night I cried myself to sleep in my dorm room. The next day, I made an appointment to talk with Dr. Gorden, the college counselor. While I cared deeply for Josh, I was tired of every date turning into a wrestling match.

I'd been praying about our relationship for weeks and

getting no answers. Josh's reactions disturbed me. I knew most guys push the limits a little every now and then, but to retreat into a dark, sullen mood afterward? I needed advice, or maybe I needed someone to tell me I was doing the right thing if I did break up with him.

At lunch Josh must have sensed my attitude change. He suggested that he drop over to the fine-arts building while I practiced. I told him I preferred to be alone. I spent the afternoon hammering out the best of Beethoven. As I prepared to leave for the counseling appointment, Josh arrived at the studio, carrying a big bouquet of daffodils. And, well, I called and canceled the appointment.

Things went smoothly between us for a few days. Josh showered me with attention. It was as if we'd somehow returned to the early days of our courtship.

During the first week of May, Josh and I drove to the recording studio to cut our demo. Besides our standard songs, we also included a couple numbers composed by Herb Cantrell, a music major at the college. The best news came when Herb's uncle, Mr. Reynolds, offered to pay for our studio time.

Vanessa arranged to meet us there. The three of us couldn't believe our good fortune. On the first and second takes, everything clicked. We completed the demo in less than eight hours. Our benefactor arrived at the studio at the close of the day. Together we listened to the raw tape and knew we had a winner. The sound engineer promised to do the final mixing and send us a final copy in a few days. He also agreed to mail one to the producer who'd requested the demo.

I can't describe the high I felt as I left the recording studio that afternoon. My body pumped so much adrenaline during the takes that I felt lightheaded and giddy. In the studio parking lot, Josh and I waved goodbye to Vanessa. I climbed into Josh's car and popped a copy of the raw cut in the tape deck. Then, with sunroof open and music blaring, we returned to campus. At the edge of town, Josh suggested we go to his apartment for a celebration meal of Italian pasta and marinara sauce. My stomach growled at the mere mention of food. We'd been so involved in the recording project that we'd forgotten to eat all day.

We worked side by side in Josh's tiny kitchen preparing the food. He fixed the pasta, and I tossed the salad. At one point, we collided at the refrigerator, laughed, and shared a kiss just as the pasta water boiled over. While I drained the noodles, Josh located two mismatched votive candles and planted them in jam jars in the center of the table. "For atmosphere," he said. Before beginning the meal, we joined hands across the table and asked God to bless our food and the demo tape.

It was like playing house. All that was missing was the marriage license. I gazed across the table into Josh's deep blue eyes. *Oh, dear Father, is this the man You intend for me to marry? I've known him for seven months, but, at this moment, I feel like I've known him for decades.* The candle melted into a puddle of wax before we moved to the sofa. We sat in the darkness in each other's arms, recalling the events of the day and sharing a few tender kisses. After one such kiss, Josh gently twirled one of my long curls around his finger.

"Summer's going to be interminable with you in Pennsylvania and me here at the college, taking summer classes."

I sighed and leaned back against his shoulder. It was as if he'd been reading my mind.

He blew the loose curls away from my ear. "I'd feel better about the separation if we had some sort of understanding. You know, Mac, you and I belong together."

"M-m-m-m." I closed my eyes, savoring his gentle ministrations.

"I can't stand the thought of your dating anyone else while you're at home." He traced his finger along my jaw line and neck.

I uttered a lazy laugh. "Oh, Josh, don't be silly. There's no one else."

"Well, you never know when another Kevin Bennett might come along."

I frowned and opened my eyes. "Kevin? Don't worry about Kevin."

Josh leaned back, his arms outstretched on the back of the sofa, the shadows enveloping his face. "Well, you two did get pretty thick there for a while."

I sat forward and studied his shaded eyes. "Josh, I don't know where you get your information." The shadows hid his expression.

Josh drew his hand away from my face. "Just how far did you go? As far as us? Farther?"

Indignant, I stood up and whirled about to face him. "That, Mr. Hanson, is none of your business. I have never and will never ask you about your old girlfriends, like Jennifer Renfro, for instance. And I demand the same respect in return."

He grabbed my wrist and pulled me down to him. "You're right. It's none of my business." He drew me into his arms and held me so tight that I found it difficult to breathe. "I just get panicky at the thought of his hands touching you. It drives me crazy!"

"Josh, let go of me. I can't breathe. Let go of me, now!"

He held me tighter. "I'll never let you go!"

Instead of crying or shouting, I quietly said, "Do you plan to leave bruises on my ribs like you did on my arms the other night?"

Instantly, he released me. He buried his face in the palms of my hands. "Why did you do it, Mac? Why did you—"

"Do what? I don't want to talk about this again." I snatched my hands away from him. "I think I'd better go."

I ran out the door and didn't stop when I heard him call after me, "Mac, wait. Mac, I'm sorry. I didn't mean to . . ." I didn't stop until I reached the dormitory. I was relieved to find my room empty. Usually Chris entertained half the female freshman population on Thursday night with popcorn and TV. Savoring the privacy, I took a hot shower and went to bed before she could come home and ask too many questions.

I tossed and turned most of the night. When I finally slept, I had a nightmare. Each time I awoke, then fell back to sleep, the nightmare returned, over and over again. In slow motion, a man wielding a giant hunting knife chased me down a long tunnel. No matter how hard I tried to run faster, I couldn't. Just as the man reached for me, I woke up. As the first streaks of dawn filled our room with light, I gave up trying to sleep and stared out the window onto the silent campus.

I should have called it quits between us. Since then, I've asked myself over and over again how I could have been so dumb. But Josh figured into so many of my dreams, especially the dream of breaking into the music world. Could I pass up such an opportunity? Except for this sex thing, so many of our goals and our dreams, even our personal likes and dislikes, meshed perfectly. I reasoned that once we were married, the sex issue would naturally resolve itself. And I did genuinely care for him.

When I prayed for guidance, God didn't answer. Later, as I shared my story with my therapist, I could see that God hadn't been silent. The warning signs were there all along. I just refused to heed them.

The next morning, Carl, Josh's former roommate, sat down across from me at my table in the cafeteria. "Josh called me last night."

"Oh?" I took a bite of toast and a drink of milk.

"He was worried about you."

I arched my eyebrow. "Really!"

Carl leaned across the table and placed his hand on my forearm. "He feels terrible over last night."

I moved my arm away. "He should."

"He really loves you, you know."

"Well, he has a strange way of showing it."

"Come on, give him a break."

We talked until the cafeteria staff chased us out of the building. He walked me to my ethics class in the humanities building. While I played difficult on the outside, inside, I knew Carl had worn me down.

Over the next few days, I allowed Josh to lure me back. It was May in the Midwest, a time for falling in love. We double-dated with Ben and Vanessa whenever Ben visited campus. And his visits were becoming more and more frequent. One weekend Ben invited all of us to the university for a student production of *Romeo and Juliet*. He arranged to have Vanessa and me stay with a cousin of his while Josh stayed with him.

With dead week on the horizon and finals immediately

thereafter, it felt good to get away from classes and labs and piano practice. On Sunday afternoon, Josh and I waited in the car while Vanessa bade Ben goodbye. In the car on the way back, she announced, "Ben asked me to marry him."

I turned in surprise. "And you said Yes?"

"Of course. We're planning a December wedding. By then, we will both be completing our last two quarters. It will be difficult seeing each other only on weekends, but anything's better than the arrangement we have now."

I shook my head. Somehow I couldn't imagine any of my friends being old enough to get married. I certainly didn't feel that grown up and responsible. At times I felt more like a girl of ten than a woman of nineteen. "But you hardly know him. You just met the guy two months ago and you're ready to spend your entire life with him?"

"Honey." Vanessa waved my objection aside. "I knew the moment I first laid eyes on him, he was the man for me! Trust me, this guy knows how to light my fire. Besides, didn't the apostle Paul say something about it being better to marry than to burn in hell?" She laughed at her humor. "Believe me, this gal's burnin' already!"

I glanced toward Josh.

He grinned. "She's got a point, you know."

"That's the most ridiculous justification for rushing into marriage that I've ever heard. My grandma always says, 'Marry in haste, and repent at leisure.' "

Vanessa touched my shoulder. "Please don't rain on my parade, Mac."

Josh glanced over the seat at her. "What if the demo goes this summer? And we need to move to Nashville to record an album?"

Vanessa shrugged. "If the unlikely happens, we'll deal with it when it comes. Ya can't plan your life around 'what ifs.' "

Silence followed. I turned back around and stared out my side window until I felt Josh's hand resting on mine. Streaks of orange, pink, and lavender filled the western sky by the time we arrived back at campus. After Vanessa got out of the car in front of the dorm, Josh coaxed me to ride with him up to Make-out Point. He'd barely turned off the engine when he asked me what I'd say if he asked me to marry him. My breath caught in my throat. Tenderly, he cupped my face with his hands and brushed his lips across mine.

All memories of his cruel accusations, our armchair tussles, and my bruised flesh receded. Fantasies of daisy chains, gossamer gowns, and candlelight dinners took their place. So often I'd imagined what it would be like the night my Prince Charming proposed to me. I glanced over at Josh's blue jeans and college sweat shirt. Blue jeans instead of royal velvet, and a Grand Am in place of a trusty steed.

I melted into his arms. As I succumbed to his caresses, I felt like a little girl acting out a fantasy with her plastic Ken and Barbie dolls, except this fantasy quickly became too real. Necking progressed to petting. At first, when his hand brushed against my bare midriff, I bristled.

He whispered in my ear, "Shh, it's all right. It's all right, my love."

I eased back against his shoulder and relaxed, allowing the surge of passion to wash over me, to engulf me with pleasure. All the while, I argued with myself that being engaged to be married made it all right. *Isn't the engagement period a time to get to know one another better? Technically, of course, we aren't engaged,* I argued. *But we're closer to marriage than we've ever been,* I recounted.

Instead of pushing his hands away, I drew them to me. The sensations I felt left me breathless and wanting more. I'd never imagined anything could feel so right. I didn't hear the car pull up beside us. And if Josh hadn't pulled away from me, I don't think I would have heard my roommate Chris banging on Josh's steamed-up window.

Josh lowered the window a couple of inches and growled, "What do you want?"

Chris peered in. If she noticed my disheveled clothing and tangled hair, she didn't say anything. "Hey, you guys. Cory and I want to go for pizza, but we don't have enough money. Would you like to go halvesies?"

"The last thing I want is pizza!" Josh grumbled, adjusting his clothing.

"Aw, come on. You guys can make out any time." I don't know how she convinced us, but we agreed to meet the two of them at the local pizza parlor in fifteen minutes.

As they drove out of the parking area, Josh leaned across me and whispered into my right ear, "Now, where were we?"

"Josh!" I pushed him playfully away. By this point, I was thanking both God and my roommate for their excellent timing. "You just told—"

"I know." He groaned, sat up, and started the car's engine. The rest of the evening and the next week, we avoided talking about the evening at Make-out Point.

With the arrival of dead week, all thoughts of recording demos, contracts, and marriage proposals took second place to practicing for my final juries and finishing the last draft for my freshman term paper. Josh needed to spend as much time as possible studying for his Greek final too. Whenever we were together, either his friends or my friends were present also.

Test week proved to be just as harried. The day before my juries, I received a long letter from Kevin, just one of many he'd written since returning to campus for spring quarter. While we'd barely spoken, he still had the strange idea we would get back together. Planning to answer his letter that night, I stuck it in my music portfolio and forgot about it.

My performance before the entire music faculty went flawlessly. Even the department chairman, who always nit-picked at his students, could find nothing significant to correct. Like a fairy princess in *Midsummer's Night's Dream*, I floated off the fine-arts concert stage into Josh's waiting arms.

He whirled me about and kissed me soundly. Startled to see him, I asked, "How long have you been standing backstage?"

He laughed and put me down. "Ever since you sat down at the piano."

"No one saw you?"

He shook his head. "Not a soul. By the way, that was a

noteworthy performance—really sharp."

I groaned and arched one eyebrow. "Involving the entire staff, right?"

He laughed. "You didn't ask me how my Greek test went."

I brushed my hand along his chin line. "So, tell me, Aristotle, how you did." I glanced down at his well-toned thighs and calves, then shot him a devilish grin. "Hmm, maybe Zeus would be a better name for you."

"Cut it out." He laughed and captured my hand in his.

"Why, Joshua Hanson, I do believe you're blushing."

He squeezed my hand. "Don't you want to know how I did on the test?"

I nodded.

"I creamed it, of course."

"Oh, of course!" I exaggerated the word *course*.

"To be honest, at first I had trouble with a few of the verb conjugations, but they came back as I worked through the questions."

"Oh, Josh, I'm so proud of you!" I looked adoringly into his eyes.

He grinned and grabbed my hand. "And now for your surprise."

"What surprise?"

"You'll see." He led me toward the front door of the music building.

"I forgot my music." I dropped his hand and ran back down the hallway. "I gotta finish up my final music theory project tonight. It's due tomorrow."

"Will it take long, the music theory, I mean?" he called after me as I ducked into the studio and grabbed my portfolio.

"Naw." I ran back to where I'd left him standing and placed the portfolio in his outstretched hand. Taking his free hand in mine, I fell into step beside him. "I just need to clean it up a bit before I run it off on the photocopier tomorrow morning."

"Good, because I have a full evening planned, but first I need to stop by the apartment and change out of these gym shorts and into more appropriate attire. After I finished the Greek test, I went over to the gym to lift weights."

"Oh." I glanced down at my pastel-pink gingham sundress. "Should I change too?"

He shook his head. "You look perfect just the way you are."

When we got to the apartment, all the drapes were drawn. He unlocked the door, and we stepped inside the darkened living room. Suddenly the lights came on and our friends popped out from behind every possible hiding place, screaming, "Congratulations!" Vanessa and Chris grabbed me and hugged me, twirling me about like grade schoolers on the front lawn.

"What is going on?" I allowed myself to be dragged across the room to the kitchen table. In the center of the table was a giant decorated sheet cake. The middle of it read "First stop—Nashville. Next stop—a Grammy!"

Vanessa grabbed both of my upper arms and danced us about the room. "It came through, Mac. The impossible happened. Mr. Harper at Gospel Records wants to fly the three of us down to Nashville in July to cut a record."

I screamed a sustained high C for what must have been a solid minute. Considering I sing low alto, that was no easy task. I turned to find Josh. He stood beside the stereo, staring at an envelope, the one containing Kevin's letter. I tugged my hands free of Vanessa's and started toward him. Oblivious to what was happening, Vanessa turned her attention to the other guests.

When I reached his side, he handed the envelope to me, his eyes crisp and cold. "It fell out of your portfolio onto the floor."

"Uh, thank you." I moved closer to him so no one would notice the sudden tension between us. "It's not what you think. There's nothing going on between Kevin and me."

Josh arched his brow, turned, and put our finished demo tape in the cassette deck. "Listen up, everyone. This is the final mix we sent to Mr. Harper."

At the sound of Josh's mellow tones filling the room, the gang quieted. My voice blended in on the chorus. While everyone except Josh glanced toward Herb Cantrell, our sophomore music-major composer, Josh walked over to the front window and stared outside. My heart ached at the pain in his face. *I'll explain,* I thought. *He'll understand after I explain.*

The last song finished dramatically. Our friends cheered and broke out the food. Josh remained aloof throughout the evening. I tried to switch back and forth from being a good hostess and playfully teasing Josh into a better mood, but I'm afraid my efforts failed on both counts. Fortunately, the party atmosphere continued without encouragement. At one point, Vanessa came into the kitchen and asked me what was wrong with Josh.

I shrugged. "Who knows? Men!"

"Yeah, men!" She laughed and returned to the parlor. Due to more final exams the next day, the party broke up early. Chris and Vanessa stayed long enough to clean up the kitchen. Josh and I worked on the devastation in the living room. Instead of improving, his mood darkened.

Sensing the strain between Josh and me, the women finished quickly and left. As the door slammed shut behind them, warning bells sounded in my head. I'd purposely avoided being alone with Josh since the drive to Make-out Point until I could sort out my own feelings for him. I knew we were in for an argument. Yet I couldn't leave things as they were between us.

I glanced at Josh kneeling beside the stereo, picking up pieces of corn chips crushed into the plush carpeting. I knelt down beside him. "Here, let me help."

We silently picked at the carpet until I could stand it no longer. I peered up into his face. "Say something, Josh. Come on," I coaxed. "We have everything going our way. Be happy."

My words fell on deaf ears. He stood and carried the crumbs to the kitchen trash can. I followed, collecting paper cups and discarded napkins on the way. Finding a small ice cube in one of the cups, I sneaked up behind him and dropped the cube down the back of his shirt. He gasped, then gyrated about, trying to catch the melting ice.

"I'm gonna' get you for that." He glared and grabbed a handful of ice from the sink.

"Try and catch me." He crouched menacingly toward me. I

screeched and ran into the living room with him less than two steps behind. As I rounded the couch, he lunged at me, but I escaped. I ran to the front door and turned the knob only to have his hand slam against the edge of the door before I could get it open. I slipped under his arm and dashed to the other side of the living room, through his bedroom, and into the bathroom. Unfortunately, so did he.

Trapping me against the sink, he dropped four or five ice cubes down the front of my sundress. He laughed while I squealed and danced. The ice fell to the floor. I bent over to pick up the pieces. When I straightened, he was gone. So was my supply of ice. I spied a plastic tumbler beside the sink, filled it with water, then tiptoed from the bathroom.

"Josh? Oh, Joshua? Where are you?" I called, playfully peering around corners and behind doors. Suddenly I heard a sound behind me. I whirled about to face him and spotted the bowl of water in his hand at the same moment he saw the tumbler in mine. With a swoosh, we were both drenched. Laughing, we fell into each other's arms. He kissed me hard.

Relieved I'd finally gotten him out of his rotten mood, I responded. As the kiss deepened, his teeth pressed into my upper lip. I could taste blood. I struggled, but he held me, pressed against his body by my neck and waist. Placing my hands on his hips, I pushed. My wet clothes allowed me to slip from his grasp.

"Oh, no, you don't!" He grabbed my wrist and whirled me around to face him. His mouth crushed down on mine once again. I couldn't breathe. An unreasonable panic welled up inside me as he inched me backward toward the bed.

I swung my head to one side. "Stop it, Josh, I mean it! You're being too rough. I'm not playing anymore."

"Come on, baby. You know you want it as much as I do," he coaxed. "You've been asking for it for a long time." Even with his head burrowed into the side of my neck, his voice sounded menacing.

"No! No, Josh. Please, please stop. You're hurting me." The backs of my calves hit the edge of the mattress. I steadied myself with one hand. Suddenly, he picked me up by my waist and tossed me onto the bed. I rolled away, only to have him haul me onto my back. When he fell on top of me, the weight of his body pushed the air out of my lungs. I struggled to catch my breath. His hands and lips were all over my neck and shoulders. Panicked, I dug my nails into his neck and into the side of his face. He pulled away. Blood oozed from the scratches.

I couldn't believe I'd done such a thing. I reached up to touch the wounds I'd inflicted. My moment of concern cost me my moment of freedom. Without warning, he resumed his attack. We tussled on the bed until he pinned my wrists above my head with his left hand and straddled my legs at the thighs.

"So you like it rough? Kevin said you were one hot item."

Kevin? I couldn't believe what he said. "No, no! We never— he never—"

Josh's mouth slammed down onto mine once again. With his free hand, he popped open the pearl buttons on my sundress and undid the front closure of my bra. I closed my eyes in shame as the cool air blew across my exposed body.

"You are so beautiful," he whispered. "A real Magdalene in the Virgin Mary's garb."

"Please, I'm begging you, Josh." I searched his eyes for compassion. Instead, I found rage. With one violent movement, his free hand ripped open the rest of my sundress.

"Did you beg Kevin to stop too? Did he tell you he'd respect you in the morning? And were you stupid enough to believe him?" He tore my underclothes from my body, and somehow, in the process, removed his own clothing. "I will, you know, respect you in the morning, that is."

"No, no! Oh, dear God, no! This isn't the way it's supposed to be!" I fought with all my strength. But my squirming excited him further. He laughed as he parted my legs with his one knee.

"And how is it supposed to be? You tell me."

With my legs temporarily free, I kicked at his sides and pummeled his back with my heels. I heard him groan with pain.

Suddenly he was groping me everywhere, unmindful of

any pain he might be inflicting. I squeezed my eyes shut and resumed my struggle to escape. I didn't see the back of his hand coming toward me. It slammed across my jaw. I heard my jaw pop to one side. My cheek stung. My jaw throbbed with pain. I tasted blood inside my mouth. He jerked my hands farther over my head until my shoulders screamed with pain.

Stunned, my eyes blinked open in surprise. "You hit me!" I screamed.

"Stop playing games!" he shouted directly in my face. He lifted his arm a second time. "And I'll do it again if that's what you want."

Through a stream of tears, I stared up into the contorted face of a stranger. "No, no. Oh, dear God, no!" Drenched in sweat and terror, I begged as he penetrated me, "Please don't hurt me . . . please don't hurt me . . ."

I closed my eyes and tried to distract myself. I tried to will myself away—far, far away to a safer place, a safer time. Somewhere beyond my agony I heard him say, "You'll like it. Honest, Mac. You'll like it."

". . . Back Where She Belonged"

JOSH

I couldn't believe it. The guy from the record company actually asked us to send him a demo.

Mac and I started dating again, thanks to the promised recording. Mac, Vanessa, and I spent every possible minute during the next few weeks rehearsing our music. When I learned of an available off-campus apartment, I grabbed it. I bought a used upright piano and had it tuned. This allowed the three of us to practice without interruptions. Most weekends, Ben drove down from the city to see Vanessa, making it a foursome. He had an open invitation to stay at my place.

When Kevin Bennett returned to campus at the beginning of spring quarter, I wondered if he'd try to win Mac back. I went out of my way to make sure he and everyone else knew that Mac and I were an item once again.

One afternoon, I went to work out in the gym. I'd just

finished a half-hour on the Nordic Track equipment when Kevin and two other gym rats showed up. Kevin strode over to the weight machine and adjusted the weights. "So, Hanson, I see you're back with Heather."

"Yeah." I wiped the sweat from my forehead.

He sat down on the bench and leered. "Gettin' any action?"

I gripped the machine's handles and counted to ten. "That's none of your business, Bennett. And if I were you, I'd keep—"

"Tsk! Tsk!" Kevin shrugged and smirked. "I'd guess you're not, by your reaction."

"Why you—" I lost it. I whirled about, ready to tear into the arrogant jerk.

Arnie, the bigger of Kevin's two friends, strong-armed me. "Back off, Hanson."

Kevin waved and laughed. "Yeah, man, I didn't mean nothin' by it. Cool down."

I swallowed my anger and headed for the showers. That evening, I guess I was still steaming because Mac and I had a stupid argument over the chorus to one of our songs. We ended the practice session early.

During the next few weeks, I struggled with images in my mind of Kevin and Mac making love. Sometimes I would get so angry that I didn't dare speak. She interpreted my silence as pouting. And I guess it was. But I resented the way she continued to hold me off and apparently permitted him to sample all the goodies.

Early on a Monday morning, Mac and I drove to the recording studio to make the demo tape. Vanessa drove her own car. I couldn't believe how well everything clicked in the studio. I'd expected that the backup and instrumental recordings would each take one day and our duets a third. But somehow, twelve hours later, we finished the last take and listened to the final cut. We were done. I guess the long hours of practice paid off. When Vanessa announced she was staying in town to do some shopping, I invited Mac over to my place to celebrate.

Pasta, candlelight, a tossed salad, and Twinkies for dessert—who could ask for more? As we worked side by side in my small kitchen, I could easily imagine what it would be like once we were married. With the dishes done, we snuggled on the sofa. Between kisses, I brought up the subject of commitment. I mean, you're always hearing the women on those dumb talk shows saying they want commitment, right?

Summer was coming. I knew that Mac planned to work in her father's office at home in Pennsylvania, while I planned to stay on campus and take a few extra classes. What if she met another jerk like Kevin Bennett while in Reading? I had to be sure she felt as committed to our relationship as I. I didn't really want her giving away any more goodies than she'd already given. Yet, even knowing better, I longed to believe her to be the pure and innocent woman of my dreams. Pure or otherwise, I'd decided she was mine. Everything was going fine until I mentioned Bennett's name.

Before I knew what had happened, I threw Bennett in her face, and she brought up Jennifer Renfro, of all people. I'd never seen Mac so mad. She would have run out the door except I caught her wrists and pulled her into my arms. Suddenly, with her body pressed against mine, all those nightmares of her and Kevin flashed across my mind. She struggled to break free, but I couldn't let go. I couldn't risk losing her—ever! In the confusion of her demanding I release her and my determination to hold on, I said more than I should have. It took a lot of fast talking and contrite apologies to keep her from calling it quits. The bouquet of flowers I gave her the next day helped too.

Things got better between us after the weekend we spent at the university with Ben and Vanessa. When Vanessa announced her and Ben's engagement on the way home, I could sense a change come over Mac. She held my hand gently as Vanessa discussed wedding gowns and bridesmaids and all that female folderol. Occasionally, she'd massage my biceps or send me a warm little smile.

When we left Vanessa at the women's dorm, neither Mac nor I wanted the evening to end. We drove up to Make-out Point and parked. We hadn't made out much since our less-than-romantic encounter at my apartment. So I decided this time, I'd take it slower so as not to blow it. As the atmosphere heated up between us, physically and emotionally, I could sense a change in her attitude. Her body was eager and receptive to my ministrations. And my body was willing and able. Even as my skilled hands urged her beyond her former limits, inside my heart of hearts, the old familiar battle raged. One part of me wanted to score, and the other wanted her to resist.

We were really going at it when Mac's roommate Chris showed up. Talk about bad timing! To tell the truth, I don't know what would have happened if she hadn't. Yes, I do. I know exactly what would have happened. And frankly, I could hardly wait. *Oh, well,* I told myself. *Next time up to bat . . .*

Heather and I barely saw each other during dead week. I had to cram for my Greek final, and she needed to practice for her last juries of the year. The letter from Gospel Records arrived in the morning mail right after my Greek exam. I wouldn't see Mac until late afternoon, after her juries. When I told Vanessa about the letter, she suggested we have a big celebration bash. She ordered the sheet cake, and I bought the rest of the food. With everything set at the apartment, I changed into gym clothes and ran over to the gym to work off my adrenaline high. Seeing Bennett shooting baskets with his friends deadened my enthusiasm. *No,* I decided, *I won't let him ruin everything this time. She's with me, not him.*

When I arrived at the fine-arts complex, the performance hall doors were locked. When the pianist before Heather came out, I begged her to let me sneak backstage and listen to Heather's performance. It was spectacular. Mac wowed the judges out of their socks, though you'd never know it by the passive expressions on their faces. They asked a few questions at the end of her third number, made a couple of suggestions, and told her she could go.

I'd never seen her look so radiant as she did walking off the stage that day. Those freckled shoulders, the pink sundress, the blush of excitement in her cheeks, her copper-brown eyes—I almost forgot why I was there. I lured her to my apartment by telling her I had a surprise for her. I unlocked the front door, and we stepped inside. Our friends sprang from their hiding places, shouting and screaming congratulations. Mac stared at me, bewildered.

I laughed and kissed her cheek. "The demo. Mr. Harper at Gospel Records liked the demo and wants us to cut an album this summer in Nashville."

"Nashville?"

Vanessa pushed between us. "That's right, honey! The three of us—isn't that incredible?" She grabbed Mac and twirled her in circles, screaming as they twirled. As they did their girl thing, I placed Mac's music portfolio on my bookcase. An envelope fell to the floor. I picked it up and read the message scrawled across the front. "To Heather, RSVP, Love, Kevin."

Pow! Someone socked me in the stomach. Nausea swept through me. Dark visions of clandestine meetings and secret rendezvous between the two of them flashed through my fevered brain. One moment, I wanted to crumble the letter in my fist, and the next, tear it into a zillion pieces. I turned and glared at the woman who betrayed me. She and Vanessa stood beside the table, admiring the cake. She glanced my way and smiled. I sent her a withering glare.

Mac glanced at the envelope in my hands, then back at me. Fear filled her eyes. She weaved her way to me. "Josh, it's not what you think. Kevin's been writing little notes—"

I shoved the letter in her hands and walked to the tape player. I was in no mood to listen to her limp excuses. I signaled for everyone to be quiet.

"Your attention, please. Here's the winning ticket that is going to take us, first to Nashville, then, move over, Take Six, we're on our way to the Grammys." I stuck the tape into the player. The crowd quieted as Mac's clear mellow alto voice filled the room, and I struggled to control my anger. At that moment, if I could have, I would have walked out the front door and never looked back. Unfortunately, it was my apartment and my party. I had no place to go. I moved through the crowd, trying to act normal, but I don't think I fooled anyone, especially Mac.

Due to test week and, probably, to my surly behavior, my guests left early. To me, the party seemed interminable. As I closed the door on the last of my guests, I surveyed the damage. What a mess! It would take me hours to make the apartment habitable again. I was grateful that Chris and Vanessa offered to help clean up the mess. Mac didn't offer, but without a word, started picking up the discarded paper plates and cups. I could hear Vanessa and Chris in the kitchen, running water in the sink. Mac and I glanced at one another amid the trash.

"Josh, I'm sorry. I can explain."

"Hmmph! Don't waste your breath." I picked up a paper cup and jammed a second cup inside it. Stale soda splashed out onto my hands. I growled under my breath and collected a handful of paper plates sitting on the table. By the time I deposited them in the trash can, Mac had gathered up the rest.

We passed in the doorway. Mac placed her hand on my arm. "I'll get a moist cloth to clean the pop off your plastic table-cloth."

We worked in silence. Sensing the tension between us, Chris and Vanessa finished the last serving dish in record speed. Chris whispered something to Mac as Vanessa handed me the soiled dish towel. "We didn't know where to put everything. Hope you can find the stuff next time you need it." She laughed a nervous laugh.

I placed a friendly kiss on her cheek. "Thanks. I appreciate your help. Let's get together tomorrow and make our plans for the summer. Have you told Ben yet?"

She shook her head. "That's what I intend to do right now." Over my shoulder she called to Heather, "See ya, Mac. Are you coming with me, Chris?"

Chris ran to catch up with Vanessa. I closed the apartment door behind the two girls. Spotting a crushed corn chip topped with guacamole dip on the carpet, I bent down to gather up the pieces and immediately found myself face to face with Mac. I inhaled the scent of her perfume. Her hair brushed against my cheek. She touched my arm and whispered some inane apology. Seething with anger, I steeled myself against the temptation to respond in kind to her. It was easy. All I had to do was picture her in Bennett's arms, his lips on hers, his hands groping . . . I stood up and turned away from her.

You aren't getting off that easy, whatever your explanation! You'll pay for carrying on with other guys behind my back, I brooded. *I'm sick of being the nice guy. If you're passing it around, I deserve a piece of the action too.* My anger grew to rage. I collected the last of the trash and carried it to the kitchen. *This is what I think of you, Bennett!* I jammed the garbage and my fist into the already full trash can. I straightened in time to feel an ice cube, cold and wet, slipping down inside the back of my shirt.

"Hey! What the—" I whirled about in time to see Heather dash for safety. Our ice fight quickly accelerated to an all-out water fight. I'm sure Mac thought we were playing. And a part of me was, at first. But in my mind, I battled a raging monster. Suddenly the monster broke loose. I grabbed Mac and crushed her against me, knowing I had to be hurting her.

I said some pretty hateful things, I guess. When she begged me to release her, I held her tighter against me. The monster I'd released scoffed at my conscience's feeble attempts to regain control even as I edged her toward the bed. When my conscience screamed at me, I shook it off with reasoning worthy of some midafternoon soap opera. *After all, we are just playing. She came on to me with her ice-cube prank. This is what she wants, right?*

We wrestled on the bed. It got pretty rough. I wanted to be gentle with her, but she wouldn't settle down. I had to hit her. When I'd had enough of foreplay, it didn't take long for me to pin her down and give her what I believed she wanted all along.

Sure, I heard her say No and ask me to stop. She had to, right? Women like to play games. But I was tired of playing silly parlor games with her. We'd been dating long enough. I had a right to expect more, considering what I knew about her and Bennett. Besides, guys have to know how to read the signals. Pretending not to want sex when she really does relieves a girl's guilt for wanting it as badly as the guy, right? I reasoned that Mac said No in order to protect her "good girl" image. *Hmmph! What good girl image?* And, if I hadn't known better, her act would have fooled even me. I had the battle scars to prove it.

First shock, then relief flooded through me when I realized Kevin had lied about scoring with Mac. *A virgin?* She hadn't slept with him or with any other man, for that matter. Guilt shoved my relief aside. I almost withdrew, except my libido demanded to be satisfied. My guilt quickly turned to anger—anger at myself, anger at Bennett, anger at Heather. *Why didn't she tell me the truth? She should have told me! If she had, I would never . . .*

With my fury and my emotions spent, I released her hands and fell on top of her. I buried my face in the tangle of fiery curls on the pillow about her head. I heard her sniffle, then whimper. *She's crying! I mean, I know I'm good, but that good?*

Suddenly reason accosted my overconfident male ego. *She's upset. Maybe I was rougher than I should have been.* I lifted up on my elbows and tried to comfort her. "Hush, honey, it's OK. I'm sorry if it hurt a little. It won't next time, I promise."

Inconsolable, she pushed feebly against my chest. "Let me go," she whimpered.

"Sure, sweetheart." I rolled off her and lay back against the pillows. With lightning speed, she grabbed the top sheet from the bed, wrapped it around herself, and stumbled to the bathroom. I heard the lock click. My ego suffered another blow when I heard her vomit into the toilet. I'd never been with a virgin before. *Maybe all girls do that the first time.* I'd heard tales of brides locking themselves in the bathroom before, but never after. And I'd never heard of a bride developing nausea as a result. I got up off the bed and knocked on the bathroom door. "Are you all right?"

"Go away."

"Well, come on out. I've seen everything ya got already."

Before the words were out of my mouth, I cringed. *That was crude, Hanson!* I pressed my ear against the door. "Sorry, Mac, I was only kidding. But we do need to talk."

"I said, Go away!"

"Heather, be reasonable."

Losing any semblance of control, she screamed hysterically, "Don't you understand English? Go away! Go away! Go away!"

"Women!" I threw my hands into the air. "OK! OK! I'll go into the living room and wait while you shower and dress, all right?"

I pulled on my shorts and padded to the kitchen for a glass of ice water. I'd just recapped the bottle when I heard the front door of my apartment open and slam shut. "Mac? Mac?" I shouted and ran to the front door, but she was gone.

"Of all the . . ." I went back into the apartment and slammed the door myself. *If she thinks I'm going to chase her up Main Street like some hero from a cheap novel, she's wrong!* I sat down on the sofa and turned on the television. *I'll give her a few minutes to get back to the dorm and calm down; then I'll call.*

Scanning through the channels, I ran across a cable rerun of my favorite Indiana Jones movie. I leaned back, put my feet up on the coffee table, and relaxed. When the mysterious blonde walked into Indy's life, I thought of Mac and smiled. I'd never seen such a sensuous female as Heather. I was already looking forward to our next sexual interlude.

During the first commercial break, I microwaved a bag of popcorn. During the second, I took a shower and started my weekly load of wash. I found Mac's underwear on the floor beside my bed. I picked it up and tossed it on top of my pile of dirty clothes.

Maybe I should give her a call now, give her a chance to apologize for losing her cool. I dialed her dorm-room number. It rang once, twice, a third time. No answer. I thought for a moment, then smiled to myself. *She must have gone somewhere with Chris, probably regaling her with the joys of the evening. Like guys, girls do that, don't they?* Hearing the movie's theme song, I returned to the living room to see the end of the film, but instead, I fell asleep on the sofa.

The doorbell jarred me awake. I don't know how long I'd been sleeping. Snow filled the TV screen. I opened the door to two uniformed police officers.

"Yes?"

"Are you Josh Hanson?" The older officer's stone face sent shivers down my spine. My first thought was that something dreadful must have happened.

"Yes, sir. What can I do for you?"

He and his partner flashed their badges at me and introduced themselves. "May we come in? We need to ask you a few questions."

I stepped back to allow them to pass. "Questions? What's happened? What's wrong?"

The spokesman of the two asked, "Are you acquainted with a young woman named Heather MacKenna?"

"Yes, of course. She's my fiancée—sort of." As I spoke, I indicated for the two men to sit down on the couch. I flicked off the television and pulled up a kitchen chair. I straddled the chair to face them. "Has she been hurt or something? Can you take me to her?"

The older man scowled. "Sort of? What do you mean, sort of her fiancée?"

"Yeah, we're sort of engaged. She hasn't technically said Yes yet, but we've talked about it." I struggled to keep my impatience in check. "Why? What's this all about? Is Mac all right?"

The police officer narrowed his eyes toward me. "Miss MacKenna is at County Memorial Hospital—"

"What?" I jumped to my feet. The younger police officer leapt up and grabbed my arm to restrain me. "Oh, dear God, no! Was she hit by a car?" I remembered her vomiting in the bathroom. "Was she taken sick? She left here less than an hour ago."

The older police officer stood and faced me. "Mr. Hanson, I'm afraid you'll need to come down to the station with us. Please don't say anything until we've read you your rights.

We are here to arrest you for the rape of Heather MacKenna."

"Rape?" My voice raised three octaves.

The younger officer hauled my arms behind my back, whipped out a pair of handcuffs, and clamped them on my wrists. "You have the right to remain silent. If you choose to waive this right, anything you say can and will be used against you in a court of law. You have the right to an attorney . . ."

I'd heard the routine on television so often I found myself reciting the statement with him. I stared in disbelief at the officer facing me. My ears rang; my head throbbed; my mind struggled to absorb the seriousness of the situation. *Mac. I gotta see Mac. She'll straighten this thing out for me . . .*

Chapter Five:

"In the Midst . . ."

HEATHER

You would think after all these years I would be able to recall the events of that day with less emotion and more self-control. It takes so little to bring it all back—a song, a girl in a pink gingham sundress, a guy with sandy blond hair, the aroma of Josh's favorite aftershave lotion. My therapist assures me that while I'll always remember the incident with pain, I'll find ways of coping with that pain. And, when I think about it, I guess he's right.

After Josh—I can hardly make myself say it even now—after Josh raped me, I ran into the bathroom and locked the door. The sheet I'd wrapped around me got stuck in the closed door. When I tried to pull it free, I spotted the stain of my lost virginity in the middle of it. I dropped the sheet in revulsion. Suddenly I felt sick, really sick. I don't know how long I wretched over the toilet. When I finally stopped, I splashed cold water on my face. I caught my reflection in the mirror.

"You fool! You stupid, stupid idiot! How could you let him . . ." *Let him? Let him what?* I asked myself. *Seduce me? No, it definitely was not seduction! Then what was it?* I glared at my reflection with disgust. "You naive, stupid girl. You got in way over your head this time!"

As I scolded the fool in the mirror, black-and-blue marks surfaced on my face and upper arms and on my rib cage. For some reason I was startled to discover I was naked. My jaw hurt. I examined it tenderly. It looked like it might be swelling.

When Josh knocked on the door and demanded I open it, I hid behind the shower curtain in fear. "Go away! Just go away!"

"You're behaving like a child. Unlock the door."

"I said, Go away!" I covered my ears with my hands to blot out his voice as well as my own.

"Look, I'm sorry. I should have been gentler with you, since it was your first time and all. But honest, I didn't know. I promise you it will be more enjoyable next time."

Next time? Next time! How can he even think there'd be a next time? Nausea welled up inside me once more. I leaned over the toilet, but nothing came. I sat back on my haunches and dried my tears. My head throbbed. I ached all over. I leaned back against the side of the tub and held my head in my hands.

After a few minutes of not hearing a sound, I pressed my ear to the bathroom door. I could hear him open the refrigerator in the kitchen. *Now! Now! Go! Go! Get out of here!* I tiptoed out of the bathroom. I covered myself as best I could with my torn dress and ran from the apartment. I didn't stop until I locked my dormitory room door behind me. I can only imagine what I must have looked like, barefoot, my hair flying in every direction, clutching my ruined dress about me. I leaned against the door and slid to the floor, sobbing. "My dress—he broke the buttons on my dress."

"What in the—" My roommate hopped off the bed and ran to me. "What happened to you? You're a mess. You look like you've been mugged or something."

I looked up at her. "My dress," I repeated; "he broke the buttons on my dress." I couldn't stop crying.

"Your dress? Forget your dress. Tell me what happened." She held me until she could get me to stop crying. When someone knocked at the door, she told them to go away.

When the story poured out of me, it poured unchecked. I don't remember telling her I'd been raped, but I do remember wanting to take a shower. I struggled to my feet. "That's what I need, a shower, a long, hot shower. I've got to wash away his touch, his filth!"

Chris grabbed me. "You can't. You'll wash away the evidence."

"But I feel so dirty. I can't stand it!" If only I could wash away the memory of the night from my mind, if only I could scrub away the scent of Josh from my body. If only, if only, if only! I heard myself screaming but couldn't stop. All the while Chris talked to me in a soft, comforting tone.

"It's all right. You're safe now. Here, let me help you remove that dress."

"He broke the buttons, all those tiny pearl-like buttons. They're ruined."

"Forget the buttons. We'll buy new ones." I remember cringing as she removed my torn dress from my shoulders.

She gasped at my bruised ribs. "Who did this to you, woman? Did you recognize the brute who did this?"

Naked and dirty, I doubled over in shame. I thought I might be sick again. Somewhere beyond the ringing in my ears I could hear Chris shouting at me, "Who did this to you? Do you think you could identify him?"

Mute, I stared at her, uncomprehending of her questions. *Of course, I can identify him. What a silly question.*

She reached for my arm. "Come on, I'm taking you to the hospital!"

Hospital? No! No! I pulled away from her and backed myself into the closet—the only dark place in the room. "No, not the hospital. No one can know about this. No one! Do you understand?"

"Heather, be reasonable. You were raped, right? That's a crime the last time I checked. So who are you trying to protect?"

I looked down at my hands. Blood stained my nails. "My nails need cleaning."

"Heather?" She touched my shoulder. I winced. "Heather! Whoever did this to you doesn't deserve your loyalty." She paused, searching my face. Suddenly her mouth dropped open. She gasped, then whispered, "Josh? Josh did this to you?"

I buried my face in my arms. My sobs came out like a series

of hiccups. *Why can't she understand?* "My dress. He ruined my sundress."

"Forget the dumb dress, will you? He got mad and raped you? Look, either I take you to the hospital right now, or I'll report him to the police right now!" She didn't wait for my answer. She marched over to my bureau, opened the top drawer, and threw a pair of panties and a bra at me. "It's your choice. Either way, you'll need to get dressed."

Like a child scolded for dawdling, I obeyed. I winced when I tried to fasten my bra. Chris came to my rescue.

"I-I-I deserved it. I made him angry."

"Deserved it? Oh, dear God! No one deserves what that creep did to you!" Chris stared at me in disbelief. "Come on, you're gonna go to the authorities. We're gonna throw the book at him."

Whimpering, I pushed my straggling hair from my face. "I can't! Don't you see? I can't tell anybody. It will ruin his future!"

She whirled me about to face her. "Ruin his future? Are you crazy? Did he think of you when he destroyed your future?" She threw her hands in the air. "I don't believe it. You're protecting that slob after what he did to you?"

A knock sounded at the door. Chris shouted, "Go away!"

Our next-door neighbor called to us through the closed door, "I have a seven-o'clock test tomorrow morning. Could you two please keep it down in there?"

Chris opened the door a crack and snarled, "No, we can not! Go eat a toad!"

I laughed in spite of myself. A sharp pain shot from one side of my jaw to the other. I could just see the poor girl slinking back to her own room. My roommate helped me to my bed. "Sit!" she ordered.

Chris walked to the closet and slid the hangers back and forth, choosing a garment for me to wear. She settled on the Hawaiian muumuu I'd worn to the January indoor beach party the college sponsored. "Here, put this on. And put on your thongs."

Meekly, I obeyed. In a strange way, I appreciated her

telling me what to do, since I couldn't get my mind to shift out of neutral. Normally, I would be furious with anyone treating me like a five-year-old. I didn't earn the nickname of "hot tamale" in grade school for being a wimp. She wadded up my soiled sundress and stuffed it into her gym bag.

"My dress . . ."

Chris sighed. "Forget the dress already! So where will it be? The hospital or the police station?"

"The hospital."

Chris grabbed her wallet and car keys and led me from the room and down the stairs to the lobby. I painfully endured the curious glances of the girls we passed along the way. I knew I looked a mess with my left eye darkening and my jaw swelling. Chris's intimidating glare warded off even the most aggressive girls' questions. When we reached the lobby, Chris hurried me past the night desk clerk.

"Don't forget to sign out." The desk clerk held out a ballpoint pen to her. "It's after midnight."

"Sign it yourself!" Chris guided me out of the building to the parking lot. I shivered as the cool night air brushed against my facial bruises. She helped me into her car, closed the door, then got in on her side.

"Maybe this isn't such a good idea, Chris." I reached for the door handle.

"You stay right where you are!" She fastened her seat belt. "And put on your seat belt! I can't afford a ticket tonight." Her authoritative tone left no room for debate. I buckled the belt as ordered, leaned back against the headrest, and closed my eyes. After a five-minute drive, we pulled into the emergency entrance of the local hospital. At the sight of the blazing neon light over the entrance way, I panicked. "Look, I feel fine. I don't need medical attention."

Chris parked the car and removed the key from the ignition. "Yes, you do. Even if you decide not to report the rape, you need a doctor to check your injuries. Who knows what damage he might have done internally? The creep!"

I took a deep breath. My mind still refused to admit that such a thing could happen to me. "It was my fault, you know.

I started it all with the ice cube."

"Heather MacKenna, that's the dumbest thing I've ever heard you say. I don't care what you did with that ridiculous ice cube, it can't justify this!" She pointed to the bruises on my arm.

Chris paused to regain her composure, then continued. "And if, after your examination, you should, in the cold light of day, decide to press charges against the slime bucket, the doctor will have collected evidence the police and the courts can use to prove your case."

"Examination? Oh, dear God, no! I-I-I can't go through the humiliation of—"

"Have you heard a word I've said?" She placed her hand gently on my forearm. "Yes, you can and you will do this. I promise I'll be right there for you, all the way."

I could feel the tears building again. "It's not you being poked and prodded and tested with who knows what. It won't be you having to answer a barrage of embarrassing questions."

"I know. And I also know that it won't be easy, but you must do it." She hopped out of the car, came around, and opened my door. I unlatched my seat belt. She helped me to my feet.

"How do you know so much about this, anyway? You act as if you've been through it yourself. You haven't, have you?"

"No, I haven't." She took my arm and led me to the entrance. I moved like a granny of eighty-five. "It's true I don't know firsthand. But my mom has been a volunteer rape counselor at a rape crisis center for the last five years."

Once inside the emergency waiting area, Chris sat me down in a chair and walked up to the receptionist's window. A man cradling a young child in his arms sat in a chair by the entranceway. Otherwise, the place was empty. The blare of the television prevented me from hearing what Chris or the woman said. Whatever it was, it produced instantaneous results. Within seconds, two nurses burst from behind the closed double doors, took my arms, and led me to a curtained area in the next room. The older nurse tried to stop Chris from following.

"Please, let her come with me. Please."

The nurse frowned. "Well, I guess she can stay until the doctor arrives. Then you'll have to ask his permission. Please hop up here on the end of the examination—"

"His?" I looked about frantically. "Isn't there a female doctor who can do this?" *A man?* I never wanted to let a man get near me again! I lunged toward the curtain. "That's it. I'm out of here!"

Chris stopped me and helped me up onto the table. I knew I was being unreasonable, but I couldn't have stopped if I tried. The nurses looked at one another. The younger one said, "Dr. Walters is on call. It would be appropriate to call her. After all, she is a gynecologist."

The older woman shrugged. "Good idea. Call the rape crisis center for a counselor while you're at it. In the meantime, I'll fill out the medical forms."

Chris handed the nurse my ruined dress, then helped me remove the muumuu and put on the paper examination robe. I sat on the end of the examination table while the nurse asked about my general health, then about the attack itself. I still fought the notion that I'd been raped. When I told the nurse that I'd dug into Josh's face and neck, she cleaned under my fingernails and carefully placed the residue in a small plastic bag. "The police will want this skin tissue saved for evidence."

"No!" I swung my head around to face Chris. "Positively not! No police!"

The nurse smiled and patted my hand. "We'll keep it just in case you change your mind, OK?"

I tightened my lips. While we waited for the doctor to arrive, one nurse took a blood test and a urine sample. The other photographed my bruises and my black eye. When the nurses left Chris and me alone for a few minutes, I tried to think of something to say, but instead, cried and pulverized one facial tissue after another.

As for Chris, she didn't stop talking. She talked about her home, her family, her thirteenth birthday party, about anything and everything. She was in the middle of telling me about a summer-camp escapade, when a thirtyish black woman wearing faded blue jeans and a teddy bear T-shirt burst into the examination area.

"Hi, I'm Dr. Walters. You must be . . ." She glanced down at the clipboard in her hand. ". . . Heather MacKenna. I'll try to make this as painless as possible for you, Heather. It sounds like you've been through enough for one night, eh?"

Dr. Walters glanced over at Chris and frowned.

Before she could object to Chris's presence, I introduced her. "Dr. Walters, this is Chris, my roommate. Can she stay with me?"

"Sure." The doctor examined the bruises on my arms and ribs. She checked my jaw. "Ooh, that must hurt," she mumbled. One quick jerk, and she popped my jaw back into place.

A crack resounded in my head. I rubbed my throbbing jaw.

"Feels better, huh? Your assailant displaced your lower jaw when he hit you. Don't eat any solid food for a couple of days. Give it time to heal."

She told the nurse to brush through my hair to collect any foreign substance such as bedding fiber or a hair from Josh's head. When it came time for the pelvic exam, I counted the dots on the Celletex ceiling. Dr. Walters's steady, soothing voice made it easier to answer the embarrassing questions.

"I noticed on the medical form that you are from Pennsylvania. I did my undergraduate work at Penn State, Philadelphia campus. However, one summer I drove to Reading every day for a class I needed that the Philly campus didn't offer in their summer curriculum."

"Really? Have you ever driven up to the Pagoda?"

She shook her head. "I wanted to, but I was always rushing to make it to class or was too tired after class to take the time."

I smiled over at Chris. She'd been right to insist I come into the hospital for a checkup. The doctor finished the exam and removed her gloves. A nod of the head by the doctor, and the nurse scurried from the room with what must have been evidence of the rape. "Have you called your folks yet?"

I sniffled and shook my head. I hadn't thought of my parents the entire evening.

"You should. They need to know. And you need them."

I nodded, but couldn't speak.

"Why don't you get dressed while I write up my findings. Then I'll take you up to my office, where you can place a call home. When the victim's advocate gets here, I'll bring her up to you, OK?"

"OK."

"Oh, yes, let's see. It's Friday morning, right? Saturday, Sunday, Monday. You need to come to our outpatient clinic on Monday for additional tests. You can make an appointment with the receptionist as you leave."

I groaned. "More tests?"

" 'Fraid so. He didn't use a condom, did he?"

I shook my head.

"And you aren't on birth control, right?"

"No."

She washed her hands and dried them on a paper towel. "Then we need to take a test for pregnancy . . ."

Pregnancy? I started. I hadn't thought of that possibility.

". . . and one for venereal disease."

I wagged my head from side to side. "That won't be necessary. I'm sure there's no chance of that. Josh is . . ."

The woman arched her brow and looked at me over her red-rimmed glasses. "You may know you're clean, but do you know every sexual partner your assailant slept with before you?"

Instantly, I thought of Jennifer Renfro. *No, she wouldn't. Or would she? What about other girls?* Josh and I had never talked about his former girlfriends, but I knew after browsing through his senior annual that he dated heavily during high school. *No,* I admitted to myself, *I don't know.* "I'll make the appointment."

The doctor readied a syringe. "Good. Now, I'm going to give you a shot for the pain. It should also help you sleep."

Calling home proved to be more difficult than I imagined. The moment I heard my father's groggy voice slur a hello, I burst into tears.

"Heather? What's wrong?" Instantly, I knew he'd awaken.

In my mind I saw him shake my mother's shoulder. "Ruth, it's Heather. She's crying. Something's terribly wrong."

Then I heard my mother's voice on the line. "Heather? Are you all right? Speak to me." In the background, I could hear my father talking about grabbing the extension phone in the den. I tried to tell her what had happened, but she couldn't understand a word I said through my sobs and my stuttering.

"Heather, where are you? Is there someone with you?"

"Ye-ye-ye-yes."

"Give them the phone."

I handed the receiver to Chris. "Hello? Mrs. MacKenna? This is Chris, Heather's roommate."

I could hear my mother shouting, "What's happened? Has there been a car accident? Is Heather all right?"

"Mrs. MacKenna, Heather's all right. We're calling you from the County Memorial Hospital. The doctor just checked her over. And she's as well as can be expected under the circumstances." Chris paused and rolled her eyes skyward. "Mrs. MacKenna, I'll be glad to, if you'll give me a chance."

Chris listened again. "Look, I don't know of any gentle way to say this, but Heather's been assaulted. No, no. A number of bruises, a black eye, a dislocated jaw, and some sore ribs." She paused. "That's right . . . Right . . . Uh-huh! . . No, she won't have to stay in the hospital overnight."

I watched Chris's face for a sign of how they were reacting. She smiled and patted my hand. "Yes, that's right, Mr. MacKenna." She paused. "Y-e-s-s, you might want to consider making the trip. . . . No, she's in no physical danger. . . . Excuse me a minute, sir." Chris took a deep breath and covered the mouthpiece. "Your dad's pressing for more information. Do you want to tell them about the rape, or should I?"

I reached for the receiver. "Daddy?" I knew I sounded like a ten-year-old. I swallowed, hoping to remove the quiver from my voice.

"What is happening up there? What is going on?" I jumped at the volume of his voice.

"Daddy, I need you." I dissolved into a fresh bout of tears. His voice softened. "Come on, puddin' head, get control."

I heard my mother's strained voice. "You're not telling us something, Heather Elaine. I can sense it."

I swallowed hard. "H-h-he—"

"Oh, dear heavenly Father!" My mother's voice rose three octaves higher than normal. "James, she's been raped! That's it, isn't it?" My sobs confirmed her suspicion.

"Heather," my father shouted, "listen to me! If we leave here within the hour, we'll be at the school before lunch." I could hear my mother sniffling softly in the background. "What filthy creep did this to you? Did you get a good look at him? Could you describe him to the police?"

My mother interjected, "Have you told Josh yet?"

"Mama," I gulped, "it was Josh who raped me." I don't know what reaction I expected, but whatever I imagined, it wasn't total silence. "Daddy? Mama? Are you still there?"

My father's words came over the line in low, deadly tones. "I heard you. Princess, would you put Christine back on for a moment, please?"

I handed the receiver to Chris.

"Yes? . . . That's right. We're waiting for a victim's advocate to get here . . . No, she doesn't want to talk to the police . . . I don't think she realizes that yet, sir." Chris listened for a few seconds. "I'll try, sir. I'll do my best."

Chris handed me the receiver. "Daddy?" I whimpered.

"I'm right here, princess." His voice broke.

"Mama, are you still there?"

"No." My father cleared his throat. "She's gone to wake your sister. Heather, please let the doctor report the rape to the sheriff."

I pressed the receiver against my ear to control the shaking in my hands. "Oh, Daddy, I'm so scared. I c-c-can't talk to a p-p-policeman about this. I'm not even sure I can t-t-tell you about it. I'm so scared."

"Heather, honey, you've done all the right things so far. Take it one step at a time. And your next step is talking with the authorities."

"I can't. Oh, God, please make the world go away!" I dropped to the floor and curled into a fetal ball on the floor.

Chris grabbed the phone from me. "Yes? Mr. Mac-Kenna? . . . Uh, I'm not sure. I'll do my best . . . No. No, I won't leave her alone, I promise."

As Chris replaced the receiver on the cradle, the doctor entered with a tiny, gray-haired woman, well into her sixties. The woman carried a huge black purse.

Suddenly feeling a little foolish curled up on the floor, I sat up and brushed my tangled hair from my face.

Dr. Walters helped me to my feet. "Heather, this is Mrs. Anna Holtzmann. She's a volunteer with the county crisis program. She's here to help you."

Mrs. Holtzmann took my hand in hers. "Heather—what a pretty name. You must be Irish, with all that beautiful red hair."

I shook my head. "No, actually my grandparents were all from Scotland."

"Ah." She nodded. "That explains the freckles." Gently she guided me toward the door. "Dr. Walters, perhaps Heather and I should go downstairs to the nurses' lounge to talk so you can lock up your office and go home for the night." Anna stared in the doctor's eyes for a moment. "Helen, are you getting enough sleep? You mustn't overdo, girl. Too many people depend on you."

The doctor smiled. "A little sleep would be nice. It's been a long day. It started this morning around four with a difficult breach delivery and hasn't stopped since."

"I'm sorry," I whimpered. "If it hadn't been for me—"

Dr. Walters waved away my objections. "Nonsense, it's all part of the package of being a doctor. You just go along with Anna and listen to her. She's a very wise woman."

As we stepped out into the hall, Mrs. Holtzmann glanced over her shoulder at Chris. "Come on, you can come too."

"Thank you, Mrs. Holtzmann," I whispered.

"Please, call me Anna."

When we entered the empty nurses' lounge, Anna suggested I make myself comfortable on the sofa while Chris lighted on the edge of one of the empty bunks. Anna plunked herself down at the opposite end of the sofa and placed her black bag on the floor beside the sofa.

At the thought of repeating my story, I felt panic building inside me. "I really don't want to talk about this anymore. I'm too tired to go through it all again." I yawned to feign sleepiness.

"That's just fine, honey. My job is to see you through the ordeal and to make sure you know your options. When you're ready to talk, I'm here." The woman opened her purse and withdrew a ball of red yarn and two knitting needles. Catching her last stitch with the needle, she sat back and started knitting.

I leaned my head against the back of the sofa. "My father wants me to report Josh to the police. Chris thinks I should too."

The woman looked at me. "What do you want to do?"

"To make it all go away."

"Besides that, I mean."

Chris smiled at me, then stretched out on the bunk and closed her eyes.

"I-I don't know."

Mrs. Holtzmann didn't look up from her knitting. "It's up to you, dear. No one will force you to do anything you don't want to do. I'm here to ensure it."

"You're not here to convince me to report the rape to the authorities?"

She shook her head. "Absolutely not. I'm on your side, and your side alone."

"But I don't know what to do." I buried my face in my hands. "I can't trust my judgment, not now, not after this."

"There's nothing wrong with your judgment, honey."

I pounded the arm of the sofa with my fist. "How can you say that? I'm here due to my poor judgment!"

Anna gazed at me for a moment. "Heather, you're here because of Josh's bad judgment. He raped you, remember, not the other way around."

"No, no! I made him angry. I should have left his apartment when Chris and Vanessa left." I whipped my head from side to side. "I should have seen it coming, with him and all his strong-arm tactics. Don't you see? I asked for it. Just like Josh said, I asked for it."

Mrs. Holtzmann's voice remained calm and quiet. "No, Heather, you're wrong. Second-guessing yourself is useless. The blame lies with Josh, not you." She cleared her throat. "No one asks to be raped. It was his decision to do what he did, not yours. He violated your basic human rights."

I dropped onto the sofa. "No one will see it that way. We've been dating for months, almost engaged, in fact."

"Heather, it doesn't matter how long you've been dating. It's your right to say No."

"But we'd been making out."

"I don't care! And neither does the law." The woman shook a knitting needle in my face. "The moment you said No and he forced himself on you, he broke the law. Remember that!"

I closed my eyes for a moment. I could hear the knitting needles clicking. "He's really a good man, Mrs. Holtzmann. I can't risk ruining his career as a minister of the gospel."

She didn't answer.

"I mean, if you knew the whole story, you'd agree." I lifted my head and looked over at her.

She continued to stare at her knitting. "So, tell me about the whole story so I can understand."

Once I started, I couldn't stop. I was surprised at the icy calm in my voice as I relived Josh's and my courtship. At one point, I paused when Chris rolled over on the bunk to face the wall but picked up the story immediately where I'd stopped. Occasionally the grandmotherly woman would give me a nod of encouragement, but mainly she just listened and worked her knitting needles.

By the time I finished describing the actual rape, I'd come to a decision. "I need to report this to the police, don't I?"

She peered at me over her eyeglass frames. "Is that what you want to do?"

"I don't know." Then I bit my lip and nodded. "Yes, I do. My dad says I have to report it."

"You're positive that's what you want to do?"

Again I nodded.

Anna placed the ball of yarn and the needles in her purse and snapped it shut. "Good. Why don't you lie down here on the sofa while I call the station house. You'll like Sheriff Hicks."

I started. "No! I can't talk to a man!"

She smiled and patted my hand. "Don't worry. He's one of the good guys, remember?"

"I-I-I don't know." My eyelids felt heavy from the sedative.

Taking my hand in hers, Anna looked into my eyes. "Heather, it's up to you. At any point, you can stop the entire process from going farther if you wish, do you understand?"

"At any time?" I smiled at the slur in my voice.

She frowned. "Well, it's true that the district attorney could decide there's enough evidence to prosecute without your consent. But that's highly unlikely. At least, I've never seen him do it. Besides, he knows I'll rap his knuckles with my knitting needles if he ever tries."

I tried to laugh, but the pain in my jaw only allowed me to grimace. Sympathy filled her eyes. She laid down her knitting and helped me over to one of the empty bunks. "Here, you sleep a while. It will take Sheriff Hicks some time to get here. He's probably over at the coffee shop downing a Danish or something." She pulled a sheet over me and tucked it under my chin. The last sensation I had was her lips briefly touching my forehead.

". . . of the Storm"

JOSH

The police officers led me, handcuffed, to the squad car. The older man opened the back door and placed his hand on top of my head. "Careful, don't bump your head."

I climbed into the car and slid to the far side of the seat. The officer slid in beside me. The younger officer hopped into the front seat. When I tried to question them about Heather, the man beside me shook his head. "I wouldn't say anything more, if I were you, until you speak with your attorney."

"Attorney? I don't have an attorney. Only criminals and

big-time financiers need attorneys."

"Well, son, I don't know where you fit in, but trust me, you need one now."

"Look, if you take me to the hospital so I can talk with Heather, we can clear this thing up in no time. I'm sure there's been a misunderstanding somewhere."

The officer beside me shook his head. "I can't do that, son."

"Well, when can I see her?"

The officer in the front seat eyed me through his rearview mirror. "Take my partner's advice. Keep quiet until you get yourself a good criminal attorney."

Criminal attorney? Me? Josh Hanson? The theology major? The future singing evangelist?

The next few hours were a nightmare. At the station, I was booked, fingerprinted, photographed, and body searched. I'd never felt so violated before in my life. Finally, one of the police officers told me I could make my one phone call. Without hesitation, I called my mother in California. Fortunately for me, she hadn't left for work yet.

When I heard her voice, I almost lost it. My voice cracked when I identified myself and told her I'd been arrested and needed her to find me a lawyer.

"Arrested? Josh, for what? Traffic violation? An accident?"

I hesitated to answer. How does a guy tell his mother that he's been booked in a jail two thousand miles away for rape? I took a deep breath. There was no way I could avoid it. "For rape, Mom."

"Rape?" she screeched. "There must be some . . . I can't . . . How? Who?"

"Mom, try to remain cool. I'm sure when I discuss this with Heather, we'll straighten it all out. But right now, they won't let me see her. And everyone's telling me that I need a good—" An officer tapped me on my shoulder and pointed at his watch. "Mom, I gotta go. Just get me a good attorney, please!"

I spent Friday night in a holding cell with two druggies, a gang banger, and a pervert arrested for indecent exposure. I found an empty cot in the corner and tried to get comfortable on the lumpy, Lysol-smelling mattress. Unaccustomed to the disgusting sounds my roommates made all night long, I couldn't get anywhere near sleep.

By dawn, my head pounded from the stress, my clothes clung to my sweaty body, and my stomach burned like cayenne pepper sprinkled on an open blister. When the guards brought breakfast trays to our cell, I took one look at the food and almost lost it. I gave most of it to my cellmates. I did drink the carton of milk, hoping it would soothe my stomach.

At eight o'clock Saturday morning, my lawyer, Mr. Robert Dodd, a balding man with a little gray hair, a comfortable pouch of a stomach, and a brisk, cynical demeanor, arrived. The guard took me to an interrogation room to speak with him. I sat down in one of the gray metal chairs and placed my elbows on the scarred and paint-chipped table.

Mr. Dodd sat down across from me. He opened his briefcase and removed a yellow legal pad and manilla folder with my name typed on the filing tab label. He made me tell my story three or four times. At various points, he would stop me to ask questions. Then he'd make notations on the yellow paper in front of him. When I thought I couldn't take much more, he read Heather's statement aloud to me. At the end, he lowered the paper and eyed me over the rims of his glasses. Stunned by Heather's accusations, I couldn't speak. My head swam; my mouth tasted like cotton. I swallowed a couple of times.

"How can she do this to me? Honest! She wanted it as much as I did." I ran my shaking fingers through my disheveled hair. "Sure, she pretended she wanted to stop, but, hey—girls always do that, right? You're a man; you know that."

Mr. Dodd narrowed his gaze. "The laws of this state interpret the crime of rape to be any forced sexual act that is accompanied by physical threat. You did hit her across the face, right?"

"Yes, I guess, but that was foreplay. I thought she wanted it rough. Some girls do, you know? Want it rough, I mean."

The lawyer took a deep breath and exhaled slowly. "Mr. Hanson, the law doesn't recognize the mental or the aberrant games men and women sometimes play with one another. If she said No, and you proceeded to have sex with her against her spoken wishes—that's rape, son."

"You mean I'm automatically guilty? Isn't there a law that says I'm innocent until proven guilty?" I pounded the tabletop with my fist. "Whose side are you on, anyway?"

"Yours, if I decide to take the case."

"What do you mean, if you decide? Isn't that why you're here?"

"I am here because an old friend from Harvard days called from San Francisco and asked me to help out his friend, your mother, I presume."

"Oh, dear God, this gets worse and worse. I can't believe this is happening to me, of all people." I buried my face in my arms. I began to shake uncontrollably. My heart raced as if I were having a heart attack. I could hardly breathe.

"Hey, I'm still here, aren't I?" His tone of voice softened. "I've decided to take your case—if it goes to court."

I looked up. "What do you mean, goes to court?"

"In cases of rape, the victim often drops the charges." His eyes narrowed into threatening slits. "But if . . ." The metalic edge returned to his voice. "If I catch you in a lie, one lie . . ." He waved a finger in my face. ". . . just one, I walk out that door, and you can fend for yourself."

Overcome with gratitude, I gulped and reached out to shake his hand. "Oh, thank you. I'm so glad someone believes my story."

The attorney ignored my extended hand and shook his finger in my face again. "Understand, I don't approve of what you did. If this Heather MacKenna were my daughter, I'd want to string you up by your—" He bit his tongue, pursed his lips, then continued. "Hanson, I'm taking the case for my friend and because I believe everyone has a right to a fair trial under the law—even rapists!"

Thoroughly cowed, I gulped and nodded. "So, what happens next?"

Dodd leaned across the small wooden table. "The detectives are going to question you about the incident. So will the district attorney."

District attorney? All the old Perry Mason reruns, the "Law and Order" shows, played in my head. Icy terror raised the little hairs on the back of my neck. When our eyes met, my fright must have shown on my face. His expression remained encased in granite.

"I'll be there with you in the interrogation room. Look to me before you answer any questions beyond your name, address—that sort of thing. Whenever your answer might incriminate you, I'll speak for you. Understand?"

I nodded.

"Stay put while I tell the detectives you're ready for questioning." Mr. Dodd stood up and walked out into the hall, closing the door behind him.

As I stared at the room's institutional green walls, the reality of my situation hit. I'd never been so scared in my life. This was no TV show where the bad guy confesses and the good guy goes free at the end of an hour. I could be convicted of a felony and spend years of my life in prison. My memory didn't need to stretch too far to recall a visit I'd made to the state penitentiary on one of our ministerial-outreach programs. I remembered feeling a trifle smug as I presented my sermonette on freedom in Jesus. I tried to picture myself wearing the shapeless orange uniforms and sitting, listening to an eager young preacher-to-be tell me that being free in Jesus makes one free indeed. I buried my face in my arms.

I sat up when I heard my lawyer greet the two detectives as they entered the room. Other than giving my name, my address, my major in school, and admitting that Heather and I were dating, Dodd declined to answer the officers' questions. When asked, I agreed to having a blood sample taken, and I agreed to take a polygraph test. I passed.

The assistant district attorney arrived by midafternoon, and I told my story once again. While the two lawyers argued over the probability of successfully prosecuting the case, I stared out the window at the new leaves on a maple tree outside the window. At one point I reminded the lawyers of the results of the lie detector test.

The assistant district attorney only grunted. "That just

means you believe you didn't rape her. A jury could look at your actions differently."

I looked over at Dodd. He lifted one eyebrow and nodded. This guy was getting under my skin. *Isn't my attorney supposed to be my advocate? Isn't he supposed to believe in me?*

My bail was set, as was the preliminary hearing date. The officials transferred me to the county jail until bail could be posted. I spent another uncomfortable night staring at the ceiling, trying to figure out what went wrong in my life. Grateful to be alone in my cell, I counted off the steps from one wall to the other, then from the bars to the back wall—8 x 8. My feet paced the cell grid as I wrestled with myself. I remembered the story of Jacob wrestling with an angel and snorted sarcastically.

No angel appeared during the long night, just a troop of frenetic demons wreaking havoc inside my skull. I began to wonder if the nightmare would ever end. Anger replaced my fear. I couldn't believe Heather would do this to me. *Doesn't she realize she's ruining my career? My entire life? Who would have thought she was that kind of girl?*

Dodd arrived the first thing Monday morning to prepare me for the preliminary hearing scheduled for immediately after lunch. "Do you have a dress suit? A white shirt and a conservative tie?"

I nodded.

"Good, wear them."

When the lawyer left, I returned to my cell, only to have the guard tell me I had two visitors. He led me back to the visitors' room. Across the room, I saw the two people I least wanted to see or whom I wanted to see me in this predicament—the two men I respected most in the entire world. I took one look at Elder Thornton, the head pastor of the college church, and Dr. Madison, the dean of the theology department, turned on my heels, and asked the guard to take me back to my cell. I couldn't stand the thought of looking into their eyes and seeing the disappointment they must be feeling.

As the guard locked the cell door behind me, my mind flashed back to the day I arrived at the college as a freshman theology major. Dr. Madison took a special interest in me. In the weeks that followed, he and his wife Gerrie made me feel completely at home, a part of their family. They had me over for special meals so often that when they went away for a weekend during my sophomore year, I dog-sat for their collie Ashes. Dr. Madison was everything I would have wanted in a father—strong, honest, straightforward, consistent.

I don't remember much about my biological dad. He walked out on my mother when I was five years old. I remember being awakened in the night, hearing my parents fighting in the parlor downstairs. I don't know what they were fighting about, but it was a doozy. I remember hearing my mother order him to leave, then running down the stairs and wrapping my arms around one of his legs and begging him to stay. He picked me up and hugged me, then told me to be a good boy and help my mama. Then he left, and I never saw him again.

A few minutes later, the same guard stopped by my cell and handed me my Bible and a note from Dr. Madison. I opened the note and read it.

"Dear Josh, we came as soon as we heard of your arrest. I understand your reluctance to see us. But, son, we came to pray with you and to offer our help through this trying time, not to condemn you. Gerrie sends her love. Your friend Carl heard I was coming to see you and asked me to bring you your Bible. I hope it will comfort you. Keep up the courage. Remember, God loves you very much. So do we. Yours in Christ, Harold Madison."

I flipped through the highlighted pages of my favorite Bible. I paused at one of my favorite verses, Jeremiah 31:3: "I have loved you with an everlasting love; I have drawn you with loving-kindness. I will build you up again and you will be rebuilt, O Virgin Israel." I continued reading. "Again you will take up your tambourines and go out to dance with the joyful. Again you will plant . . ."

Tears filled my eyes. My breath caught in my throat. If only I could believe the promise I read. My life was in shambles. I'd been betrayed by the woman I'd asked to be my wife. I was embarrassed beyond belief. Even if I were cleared of all charges, I was ruined. I slammed the book down on the mattress beside me. "God, where are You?"

One of my cellmates rolled over on his bunk and growled, "Shut up!"

I stood up, walked to the bars, then back to my bunk.

"All right, Hanson, grab your book. You're out of here. Someone posted your bail." The guard unlocked the door and motioned for me to follow him.

"Who?" I asked. "Who paid my bail?"

The guard shrugged and unlocked the outer door. "Some woman named Vera West."

"My mother? My mother's here?" I couldn't believe it. Finally, someone on my side! But then, she'd always been on my side. I could hardly stand still as the guard unlocked the cell and led me to the waiting area. When he opened the last door, I burst through the doorway into my mother's waiting arms.

The scent of her perfume and the feel of her arms around my waist—a strange flood of emotions swept over me. It was like I'd become a schoolboy again. I choked back the tears welling up in my eyes. Reluctant to let go, afraid that her presence was no more than a dream, I held her for some time. I felt rather than heard the sobs coming from her.

"Mother, are you all right?" I pulled back and searched her tear-stained face. "It's going to be OK, you know. All we have to do is talk with Mac. She'll clear things up in no time."

Mom didn't speak. She just shook her head and walked toward the exit. I watched her walk away.

"Mom, wait up. What's wrong? It's just a misunderstanding, really." I followed her to the parking lot, trying to get her to say something—anything!

In spite of my best efforts, she didn't talk on the ride back to my apartment. The tears glistening in her eyes ripped my insides apart. I couldn't stand having her shut me out. How could she, at a time when I needed her strength more than ever? Disappointed, I avoided looking at her. I didn't want to lose it in public.

I unlocked the apartment door and ushered her inside. It

was the first time she'd seen my place. Normally I would have been proud of it. But that day, everywhere I looked I saw Mac—Mac cooking pasta in the kitchen, Mac picking up corn chips off the carpet, Mac curled up beside me on the couch, Mac . . .

I looked around the living room, then glanced into the bedroom at the bare mattress. My pile of unwashed laundry sat beside the bathroom door, but Mac's underwear was missing. "Someone's been in here," I mumbled. *But, of course, this is supposedly a crime scene. I guess I should be thankful the place looks as good as it does.*

I sensed my mother standing beside me. I turned toward her, following her gaze to the unmade bed. My face reddened with shame as I saw the room through her eyes. I put my arm around her shoulders. "Mom, it wasn't like they are saying. Mac wanted—"

"Oh, spare me, Joshua!" She looked up into my eyes. I could see a blend of disappointment, frustration, and disgust. She shook her head and walked to the living room. I followed her.

"Mom, ya gotta believe me. I didn't rape Heather."

At the doorway between the parlor and the kitchen, she whirled about to face me. "Josh, I don't know what to say to you. I don't know how to feel. I love you. You're my only child." Tears spilled down her cheeks as she clasped one hand over her mouth to stifle her cries. "Yet, at this moment—oh, dear God, I never thought I'd hear myself saying this—when I look at your face, I feel total revulsion and shame."

My mouth dropped open. *Mama?*

She cleared her throat. "I'm sorry, Josh, that I can't be more supportive of you, but I loathe you for what you did to that girl!"

I rushed toward her, gesturing with my arms the helplessness I felt. "But, Mom, that's the point. I didn't do what she claims, honest."

My mother wrapped her arms about herself. "Oh, Josh, how could you do such a thing? Where did I go wrong as a mother that you would have so little respect for a woman as to force—"

I took hold of her upper arms. "Mom, no! No! It's not your fault. If there's any blame it's Heather's, and mine."

Fury filled her eyes. She jerked away from me and shook her finger in my face. "Don't you dare blame the poor girl for your disgusting sin."

I cringed before her anger. "B-b-b-but—"

"She may have made a mistake to trust you, but you! You—"

I shook my head vehemently. I couldn't believe it. *This is my mother talking?* If my own mother didn't believe in my innocence, how would I ever convince a judge and a jury? "Mom, you don't understand."

"No! You don't understand. I met with both the assistant district attorney and with Mr. Dodd, the lawyer my boss asked to represent you. They let me read the hospital report. The girl begged you to stop, but you didn't!"

"Mom, be reasonable. Mac didn't mean it. Honest. All I can figure is that once she got back to the dorm she felt guilty about us having sex and all and made up this rape story to make herself feel better."

At that point, my mother pushed me away from her with such force I backed into the stereo. She stormed to the front window and looked out on the busy street for a few seconds. "Just tell me, Josh, yes or no. Did the girl try to stop you?"

I swallowed hard. "Yes, but—"

She whirled about to face me. Disgust distorted her usually gentle features. "The law calls what you did rape! Plain and simple! It's rape if she prosecutes. It's rape if she doesn't. Rape is rape! It would be rape if neither of you never told a soul."

"Mother, you're supposed to be on my side."

"Oh, Joshua! I love you with all my heart. But I can't—I won't excuse your sin against this girl! Just listen to yourself, blaming her for your lack of self-control. You hit her, you one hundred seventy-five pound brute, you hit her!"

"I-I-I do feel bad about that." I pulled my shirt collar away from the scratches on my neck. "And I suppose it doesn't matter that she did this to me."

"Deliver me!" My mother rolled her eyes heavenward.

"Consider yourself lucky, son. If I'd been Heather, I would have gone for your eyes!"

"Mother!"

"Hey, I've been a woman alone long enough to learn a few techniques to protect myself from men like you. How would you be feeling right now if I were in Heather's place, if I'd been the victim of some man's violent lack of self-control?"

"Mom, no man would—" She silenced me by arching one eyebrow. Suddenly, for the first time, I saw my mother as a woman, a woman battling the world alone after the loss of her first husband. Then enduring the abuse of a second marriage until divorce was the only answer. I'd never thought about her in a sexual situation, I guess. She'd always been just Mom to me. Oh, of course, I knew she was a female, but I'd never seen her as a woman men might come on to. And I didn't like the thought.

My mother walked into the kitchen and opened the refrigerator door. "You must be hungry. Can I fix you something before we leave for the courthouse?"

I mumbled something about taking a shower and stumbled into the bathroom. As the hot water pulsated against my shoulders, I told myself the situation with Mac and me was different. *We love one another, or at least, we did. It's really Kevin Bennett's fault. If he hadn't led me to believe Mac was loose, I never would have expected her to put out—at least I wouldn't have been so angry with her for not wanting to—*I froze. *Not wanting to . . .* I shook the thought out of my head. *No! She wanted it as much as I. I know she wanted it!*

I pounded my fist against the tiled wall. *No one can convince me Mac didn't want to have sex just as badly as I did. Why else would she have hung around after the party? And what about the little water fight and the ice down my shirt? I mean, talk about asking for it!*

I turned my face into the spray. The water pelted my flesh. I grabbed the soap and sudsed my face. My stubbled beard scratched against the palms of my hands. I winced as my fingers brushed over the scratches on my face and neck. *Boy, the little wench really did a number on me.*

Like a CD permanently set on repeat, I heard my mother's voice. "Deliver me! If I'd been Heather, I'd have gone for your eyes! Rape, Josh. You raped her! Rape, Josh. You raped her! Rape, Josh. You raped . . ."

"No, No. I didn't rape her. I didn't rape her! Oh, God, please tell me that I didn't rape Heather!" Heather's frightened and distorted face appeared before me—the look she gave me just before she locked herself in the bathroom. Her lips moved, but no sound came from her mouth. It didn't need to; I knew what she was saying. "You raped me! You raped me! You raped me!"

"No! No!" I pounded my fists against the wall and slammed my forehead against the shower tiles. "No! No! I didn't. I didn't. I didn't!"

My cries echoed off the shower walls, physically accosting me from every side. "No! No! I didn't rape her! I didn't!"

Feeling sick to my stomach, I doubled over. I could hear Heather retching and retching. "Oh, God, make her stop! Please make her stop!"

As my own words pummeled me, I slid down the wall into a sitting position on the floor of the stall. Lukewarm water replaced the hot spray, but I hardly noticed. I heard a knock at the bathroom door.

"Josh, are you all right? Josh, answer me!"

I must have answered, because she went away. I could still hear myself whimpering, "No, no, I didn't rape her." I leaned my head back and let the now-cool water wash over my face and shoulders. As the water pulsated against my flesh, a silent video of the fateful night flowed through my mind. I watched two strangers, a man and a woman, acting out a love scene from what had to be an X-rated Sunday-night movie. A love scene? No. Hardly a love scene. The man was too intense; the woman too frightened. She struggled to break free of the man's grasp. She begged him to—suddenly I knew. I didn't hear any voices other than my own. No booming bass out of heaven accused me of my sin. No ringing gavel declared me guilty, but I knew. I'd been fooling myself. *It's true. Mac wasn't playing games. She begged me to stop, and I didn't. I really did rape Heather MacKenna!*

My mind staggered from the knowledge. I'd damaged the most beautiful creature in my life. *Will she ever forgive me?* I felt a sharp pain in my chest. My throat tightened till I couldn't swallow. I felt like I'd been mud wrestling and allowed the mud to dry on my skin. In spite of the water cascading down on me, I felt filthy.

People talk about out-of-body experiences. That's how I suddenly felt, out of my body, looking down on this ugly, despicable creature. Desperate to wash away the dirt and the filth embedded in my soul, I scrambled to my feet. I grabbed the cake of soap and a washcloth and scrubbed until my flesh was red and sore. Yet I felt no cleaner than I had before. A loud, agonizing wail erupted from deep inside me. The cry filled the shower stall. "Oh, God, forgive me. Please, oh, please, forgive me. I'll do anything for You, if You'll just forgive me."

Exhausted, I turned off the faucets and stepped out of the stall onto the bathmat. I turned toward the mirror over the sink, but steam obliterated my visage. Taking a towel from the rack, I rubbed away the steam and saw the face of a rapist. Quickly, I turned away and dried off.

I remembered the story of King David and Bathsheba. While the Bible doesn't call their act rape, it was mighty close, considering his power and position as her husband's commanding officer. He did make her an offer she could hardly refuse. Then I recalled the prophet Nathan's visit to David. How ironic that my Nathan would be my own mother!

The words of David's prayer in Psalm 51 came into my mind. I'd read the words so many times, even memorized them once. But there, in the middle of my 4 x 4 bathroom, the words took on new meaning. "Have mercy on me, O God, according to your unfailing love; according to your great compassion blot out my transgressions."

I dried my chest and back. "Wash away all my iniquity and cleanse me from my sin. For I know my transgressions, and my sin is always before me." I continued reciting the prayer as I dried my legs and feet. "Cleanse me with hyssop, and I will be clean; wash me, and I will be whiter than snow."

Whiter than snow? O God, is such a thing possible? Now? After everything that's happened? "Create in me a pure heart, O God, and renew a steadfast spirit within me." I'd known this once. Once I wouldn't ask if forgiveness was mine. Now, I wasn't so sure.

I gave myself a punishing stare in the mirror. A string of epithets flooded through my mind. For the first time in my life, I saw myself as the "filthy worm" about whom the hymnist wrote instead of the royal son of God. *God? God? Where did I lose the sense of Your presence, Father? Once I was committed to You. But I guess that's over. Once I was clean and proud to be called Your son. Once I believed the Spirit had called me to Your service. What a joke, huh?*

Jeremiah 31 comforted my exhausted mind. "I have loved you with an everlasting love. . . . I will build you up again. . . . I will forgive [your] wickedness, and remember [your] sins no more. . . ."

My face blurred before my eyes. For the first time in my life, I couldn't deny my guilt. For the first time, there was no one to blame. I stood facing my own reflection and hating it. Oh, I'd repented of my sins before, but always with an arrogance, a feeling that God would forgive me because of who I was. After all, hadn't I decided to dedicate my entire life to His work? Hadn't I, like Moses, rejected the pleasure of Egypt to serve my God? Wasn't I one of His chosen?

I stared at the face in the mirror—not the leering face of the rapist Heather saw towering over her, or the arrogant, indignant face Mr. Dodd saw in the interrogation room, but the ashen face of a convicted criminal standing before an angry God.

"Oh, Lord, I don't deserve Your forgiveness. I don't deserve Your love. I'd be a hypocrite to even ask." Like a CD recording from God's throne room, the psalm replayed through my mind. The words were more a confession than a recitation. This time the prayer exploded out of me, unchecked, from the deepest part of my soul. *"Do not cast me from Your presence or take Your Holy Spirit from me. Restore to me the joy of Your salvation and grant me a willing spirit to sustain me."*

Chapter Six:

"Though I Walk . . ."

HEATHER

Sheriff Hicks burst into the room with the force of a Sherman tank. Suddenly my life, my thoughts, my future were no longer my own. Mrs. Holtzmann introduced the 6'4", 250-pound former college quarterback with the game leg and the bushy brown mustache by his given name, Harold. The mere sight of Harold terrorized me. It must have shown in my face.

"Now, sweety," Anna began, "Harold here is as gentle as a Saint Bernard. He won't bite, I promise." She glanced over at the hulking giant. "If he tries, I'll make him heel!"

I couldn't help but laugh at the image of the 5'2" granny restraining the sheriff with only her set of knitting needles. Anna winked at me. "Harold and I go back a long way."

The director of nurses escorted the four of us to an empty office where we could talk without interruptions.

"I don't know about this," I whispered to Chris, eyeing the sheriff with mounting distrust. "I don't think I can go through with this."

She tipped her head toward Anna. "You don't have to, you know. At least that's what Mrs. Holtzmann said."

"Hey, you were the one telling me to report it, remember?"

"I admit it." Chris shrugged. "I don't think Josh should get away with hurting you as he did. Who knows who his next victim will be if you keep quiet?"

I frowned. I hadn't thought of future victims. In the office, the sheriff chose to sit in the straight-back office chair while Chris and Anna sat beside me on the leather sofa.

Telling my story to the burly police officer proved to be worse than I'd imagined. My face flamed as I described each of Josh's actions. Fortunately, when I related the more delicate moments, the sheriff scribbled down notes in his small note pad instead of looking at me as I spoke. Whenever he preceded his questions with, "I know this isn't easy for you, Miss MacKenna," I stiffened and choked back the tears that constantly brimmed in my eyes.

"There are a number of questions I have to ask. Please don't be offended. Just tell the truth as best you can." Noting the threat of tears, he spotted a box of facial tissues on the desk and handed it to me.

"Thank you," I whispered.

"Miss MacKenna, would you tell me again what transpired between you and Mr. Hanson from the point of the water fight? Slowly, please."

Anna bristled. "Does she have to tell it all again, Harold? It's been a rough night."

The sheriff swallowed hard. "Sorry, Anna, it's important. You know the rules."

Through tears, hiccups, and sniffles, I did as I was told. When I reached the point where I ran from the apartment, he stopped me. "That's fine, Heather. May I call you Heather?"

I nodded.

"I want you to search your heart before you answer my next question." He paused and looked down at his notepad. "Are you sure that you aren't claiming rape to ease your conscience for having sex with your boyfriend? Or because he made you mad about something?"

I glanced at Chris, then at Anna. "I-I-I don't know. I honestly don't know. Maybe I should have fought harder. I don't know." I clapped my hand over my mouth to stifle my sobs. "I can't do this anymore."

He persisted. "Are you sure you made it clear to Joshua that you didn't want sex?"

My face flamed again. "Yes! Yes! I begged him not to—to . . ." I stared at the mutilated facial tissue in my hands.

"Did you try to fight back?"

Mrs. Holtzmann leapt to her feet. "Harold, I'm ashamed of you! Would you ask the victim of a mugging if he fought back? Would you imply that he was partially guilty of the crime by allowing himself to be robbed?"

"Anna." The officer sighed and shook his head.

"Well, would you? I mean, the victim of a mugging might have been guilty of a bad decision to walk through a certain part of town at night, but that doesn't make him guilty of causing his own mugging!"

The sheriff shook his head again. "We're not talking mugging here, Anna."

"Hmmph! Well, you should be. Doesn't a rape victim deserve the same respectful treatment granted a victim of theft or, or whatever?"

"Anna, sit down! Please, Miss MacKenna, if you don't mind, would you answer my question? Did you try to fight off your assailant?"

I nodded. "I scratched his face and neck."

The sheriff avoided looking toward Anna. "Scratches are often made in the heat of passion, Heather. Some couples enjoy it rough."

"Harold!" Anna glared at the police officer.

"Look, I'm sorry, but I have to be sure she's telling the truth, or the department could be sued for false arrest."

Mrs. Holtzmann clicked her tongue. "You do recall, don't you, that Heather did not perpetrate this crime against herself? She didn't wear a sign that said, 'Rape me! Rape me!' "

The sheriff shook his head in disgust. "Anna, Anna, Anna! If it were anyone but you, I'd have my deputy throw you out of here on your ear. You, of all people, should know that the questions the defense attorney will ask in the courtroom will be a lot more degrading than anything I might ask her in the privacy of this room."

With growing apprehension, I listened to the exchange

between the victim's advocate and the officer. He was right; I knew it. *Do I really have to go through with this?*

I leaned back against the couch and stared up at the ceiling. In the background I could hear Anna and Sheriff Hicks discussing me as they might a five-year-old. If only I could will myself away—escape the nightmare of the last twelve hours.

I closed my eyes and pictured myself walking beside my dad along the Schuylkill River. I smelled the pungent aroma of blossoming honeysuckle growing along the banks of the river. Overhead, a wispy jet trail cut across the cobalt blue sky. I could see my mother walking on the other side of Dad and my little sister running ahead of us, searching for the perfect stone to skip in the river. My mother called to me. "Heather? Heather!"

"Heather? Heather!" Anna shook my arm. "Heather? Are you all right?"

I grimaced as my idyllic daydream vanished and the cold, hard reality of the hospital office returned. *Oh, dear Lord, I'm not sure I can go through with this.*

Sheriff Hicks stood up. "Heather, I think I have enough to go on for now. Anna here has suggested that Chris take you back to the dormitory until your parents arrive from Pennsylvania. In the meantime, try and get some sleep, OK?"

I nodded.

On the way back to school, I remembered that I'd have to walk past people I knew in order to reach my room. "Chris, stop the car!"

"What? What happened?" My sudden command came with such force, she jammed on the brakes. A Dodge 4 x 4 screeched to a halt behind us. The driver gestured angrily and swerved out around us.

"Chris, I can't go back to the dorm—ever!"

"What do you mean? Where else would you go?"

"I don't know." I shook my head violently. My breath came in short, desperate gasps. "I-I don't know, a motel maybe, at least until my parents get here."

"A motel?" She took a deep breath. "But I gave the sheriff

and Mrs. Holtzmann our phone number in case they needed to reach us."

"So give them the motel's phone number!" I shouted in her face. "I can't! I won't go back to the dorm!"

Chris threw her hands in the air. "All right. All right. To a motel it is. Do you have a preference as to the motel?"

"Somewhere cheap!" My fury spent, I withered down into a clump of raw nerves.

Stepping on the gas again, she turned the next corner. "Do you have any money on you?"

I shook my head.

"Neither do I. Wait, I have my mom's ever-ready, trusty credit card."

I sniffled, then blew my nose. "I'll pay you back, I promise."

She reached over and patted my knee. "I know. Let's not worry about that right now. Let's just get you into a shower and to bed."

A shower! I'd forgotten about the shower. *Oh, yes, I need a long, hot, punishing shower.*

"Are you hungry? I can stop at—"

Bile rose to my throat. I shuddered. "Oh, no. The mere thought of food sends my stomach into a forward roll."

"Well, I am. It's been a long time since . . ." She didn't finish her thought. She didn't have to. The infamous celebration party flashed before my eyes. "I'm sorry."

"Just get me to a motel, please," I whispered.

Chris nodded, pointing out her side window. "There's one." She veered the car into the parking lot and killed the engine. "I'll go register for us. You stay right here. Will you be OK?"

"Yes, I think so."

Once inside the sparse but clean motel room, I headed for the shower. When Chris offered to help me remove my clothes, I suddenly became embarrassed. "N-n-o, I can do it."

"Are you sure?"

I nodded. "Look, while I'm taking a shower, why don't you go and get yourself something to eat?"

She shook her head. "I promised your dad I wouldn't leave you alone."

"I'll be fine, really. Just go get yourself a taco or something. Bring me back a, a diet 7UP, OK?"

"Good suggestion. If you think you'll be OK alone here for a few minutes, I can swing by the dorm and pick up a few things for you."

What if Josh comes for me? What if he finds me here? I took a deep breath. *Be reasonable, Heather. He has no way of knowing where you are.* "I'll be just fine. You go ahead."

"Are you sure?" She placed her hand on my arm. I winced. "Oh, sorry."

"I'll be fine, really." *You'd think I was a porcelain doll that had been dropped on its head, the way she's mothering me.* I turned and pushed her toward the door. "Go. I'll be perfectly fine. Here, take the key with you. I'll probably be asleep by the time you get back."

She laughed. We had a standing joke about Chris's dramatic entrances into a room, a virtual tsunami wave. "All right. All right! I'll go. Here's the card Mrs. Holtzmann gave me before we left the hospital. Call her if you need someone while I'm gone."

I laid the card on the desk, opened the door, and pushed her through it. "I'll be fine, just fine. Away with you."

Chris laughed and ran to her car. "I'll be back in no time, you'll see."

I waved her away. "Go!"

As she drove out of the parking lot, I slipped back inside the motel room and securely locked all the locks on the door. When I realized Chris would have trouble releasing the chain lock, I undid it. A shiver coursed through me as I gazed about the darkened room. Suddenly it was quiet, too quiet. *"Heather, get a grip on yourself!"*

I switched on the television set full-volume. A voluptuous blond starlet, her dress barely clinging to her, giggled and batted her Elizabeth Arden eyelashes as a talk-show host asked her about the release of her newest movie.

When he asked her why the movie rated an R, she arched her upper body suggestively. "Obviously there's a little sex and a little violence in it. [giggle, giggle] To please the public, you know. However, to me the story line makes a definitive statement against—"

Very good, a four-syllable word. Quite a stretch for an airhead whose dryer is permanently set on fluff!

"—the public's fascination with violence against, and exploitation of, women."

I clicked my tongue. "Right! And you aren't contributing to that fascination?"

"Let's let the audience decide for themselves, shall we?" The sarcastic talk-show host smiled at the camera. "Roll the clip from the movie."

Disgusted, I entered the bathroom, shed my clothes, and stepped into the shower. I fumbled with the miniature bar of soap I found on the soap tray. My fingers shook so much I couldn't open the wrapper. *Stupid packaging!* Frustrated, I stepped out of the shower and ran to the desk, opened the center drawer, and found a letter opener.

Returning to the shower stall, I turned on the water, then attempted to unwrap the soap by force. The wrapper fluttered to the floor as I stepped into the shower and turned my face into the cool spray. Soap in one hand and the letter opener in the other, I adjusted the water temperature to hot. It felt good to have the hot water batter my face and chest. *Clean, I just want to feel clean again.* In the background I heard a threatening male voice.

Suddenly, a young woman screamed, "No! No, don't do this to me, Johnny. Put down that knife. Johnny, I'm sorry. I'm sorry I wasn't here when you called. Stay away from me!"

"Millicent, I know where you were and who you were with. You will pay."

"No! No! I'm sorry; I'm sorry! Stay away from me. Please, please, don't hurt me!"

In my sleep-deprived mind, the dialogue shifted. Josh replaced Johnny, and I saw myself on the bed, pleading for mercy. I stared into the stream of pulsating water. I felt lightheaded. My world begin to spin in circles. Round and round I spun, whirling out of control. I tried to steady myself against the walls of the stall.

Josh's face, contorted with anger, came toward me, pressing me against the wall, squeezing the very breath out of my lungs. I heard Millicent screaming and screaming and screaming. I covered my ears to escape her bone-chilling screams. *Stop! Stop! Oh, please, God, make her stop screaming!*

I heard a stranger shout at the actress, telling her to stop screaming. *Yes, yes,* I thought. *Make her stop screaming!* I can barely remember the unfamiliar face of a police officer peering down at me from beyond the shower walls or the two pairs of strange hands lifting me out of the shower or a woman wrapping a blanket around me, covering my naked body.

Somewhere in my memory, I remember Chris holding me, comforting me—or at least, I think I could if they'd only turn off that stupid television, if only they could make that dumb blonde stop screaming. Before I drifted off into a downy white cloud of silence, an ambulance siren overrode the woman's screams.

When I opened my eyes, I found Dr. Walters leaning over me, prying my eyelids open, poking at me, calling my name. I smiled at the hazy halo circling her head. *Like an angel, just like an angel.*

"She's coming to. I think she's going to be just fine. Why don't you wheel her up to the room while I talk with her parents?"

Room? No, I can't go back to my dorm room. Everyone will know what happened! Everyone will blame me. It's my fault. It's all my fault! I struggled to sit up, but something held me fast.

"No, Heather. You're OK. Everything's OK."

"Where am I? Don't take me back to my room. Please, I can't go back to my room."

"Heather, calm down, everything's fine. It's me, Dr. Walters. You're in the hospital."

"Hospital?" I tried to focus my eyes, but the room refused to quit spinning. "Chris, I told Chris—"

"Sh-sh-sh. Chris is waiting in the lobby with your parents."

"My parents? My folks are here?" I tried once again to get off the table. I glanced at my incapacitated left arm, then at my right. I craned my neck to look down toward my feet. Leather straps bound my wrists and ankles fast to the gurney. Defeated, I sank back against the rigid surface. "Dr. Walters, I need to see my daddy. Please let me see my daddy."

"You will, I promise. In a few minutes, after the nurses get you settled into a room upstairs, I'll send both of your parents up to see you."

An orderly wheeled me to my room with dizzying speed. After removing the restraints from my wrists and ankles, he and a middle-aged nurse lifted me onto a bed. The nurse immediately strapped me down once more.

I looked at her in surprise. "Are these necessary?"

She showed no emotion as she hung an IV bag from the pole beside my bed and injected a needle in my wrist. "Until Dr. Walters instructs otherwise. Now, now, young lady." She glared at me. "I won't tolerate any of your suicide nonsense on my ward."

"Suicide? Me?" I stared at her in disbelief.

Adjusting the flow of liquid from the bag, the woman tightened her lips and frowned at me. "I can't understand how anyone could attempt to end their life when others fight to sustain theirs." Without another word, the grim-faced woman turned and left the room.

Confused, I gazed about the room. Except for the screen mesh covering the window, it could be any hospital room I'd ever seen. I noticed the call button clipped to my pillowcase. *A lot of good that thing will do with my hands tied to the sides of the bed! Obviously, there's nothing I can do but wait for Dr. Walters to explain to me what's happening.* Frustrated, I closed my eyes. I must have slept for some time, since I awoke to the late-afternoon sun shining in my eyes. I rolled my head to the other side and opened my eyes.

"Mama? Is that you?"

"I'm right here, princess." My mother reached out and brushed the stray curls from my forehead.

I tried to reach out to her. My hands were still tied down. "Oh, Mama, I'm so glad to . . ." I dissolved into a flood of tears.

She leaned over and gathered me as best she could into her

arms. "It's all right, darling. You're safe now."

I inhaled the sweet scent of my mother. She and her Wind Song perfume. "Oh, Mama, I'm so ashamed."

I felt her warm breath on my neck. "No, no. Sh-sh-sh. It's OK. Everything's going to be all right."

"Nothing will ever be all right again!" I wailed, casting my face away from hers.

"I know it seems that way right now. But you'll heal, you'll see." Drawing back, tears filled her eyes as she caressed the bruises on my arm and ran her hand along the side of my face. "My poor baby . . ." A sob caught in her throat.

I turned back to face her. "I want to go home, Mama. Today! I want to go home."

She forced a smile. "As soon as possible, I promise."

I glanced about the room. "Where's Daddy? Didn't Daddy come?"

Her smile widened. "Of course he did. Do you think I could have kept him away? He's down at the police station."

The police station. Sheriff Hicks! The nightmare returned.

"René and Chris went to the dorm to pack up your things. Chris said you didn't want to return to the dorm, is that right?"

I nodded.

"A Mrs. Holtzmann stopped by a while ago to see if you needed anything. She seems like a nice old lady."

"She is." I closed my eyes once again. I couldn't believe how tired I felt.

My mother continued talking. "She volunteers her time as a victim's advocate. Did she tell you that five years ago, two teenage boys broke into her house and raped her?"

My eyes flew open. I stared at her in surprise.

"That's right. She understands all too well how you feel right now. She said she'd be back during visiting hours tonight." My mother talked on, but my thoughts refused to follow her.

Visiting hours? How long will I be stuck in this place? How much longer will this ordeal continue? I closed my eyes and fell asleep to the sound of her voice.

Except for momentary awakenings from the surrealistic nightmares, I slept until dawn the next morning. I opened my eyes to find Mrs. Holtzmann asleep in the armchair at the foot of my bed. I tried to speak. My mouth tasted bitter from the drugs I'd been given. "Mama?"

"Sh-sh-sh, it's OK, Heather. You're safe." Anna rushed to my side. "I sent her back to the motel to rest for a few minutes."

Shh! Unreasonable anger welled up inside me. *Why does everyone keep shushing me?*

"I'm so thirsty." I slurred the *r* in *thirsty*.

Mrs. Holtzmann touched a plastic straw to my lips. I greedily sipped the deliciously cold water. "You must be hungry too," she said. "Let me have the nurse bring you a bowl of gelatin or something." She pushed the buzzer attached to my pillowcase.

I thought for a moment. My stomach growled. *Food? That does sound good.*

Almost instantly, a nurse appeared, took Mrs. Holtzmann's order, and returned with a small bowl of cherry-flavored gelatin. The nurse freed my left hand so I could feed myself. I sipped on the cool, sweet dessert while Mrs. Holtzmann related the events of the last two days.

"When a traveling salesman reported a young woman screaming in the unit next to his, the motel manager called the police. On the way to the motel, the police officer called for an ambulance. Chris arrived just as the manager unlocked the motel-room door for the police. They found you huddled in the corner of the shower stall with scalding water pouring down on you. You held a letter opener in your hands and were screaming for all you were worth."

"I don't re—"

"I know. I know." She patted my shoulder. "Do you want me to go on?"

"Yes," I whimpered, staring at the gelatin jiggling on the spoon.

"Thinking you'd tried to commit suicide, they brought you to the emergency room. You were in shock. Dr. Walters asked that you be admitted for observation."

"And this?" I gestured toward the IV in my right arm.

She shrugged. "I presume it's something to stabilize your blood sugar and your system."

"I didn't try to kill myself, you know. I can't say the idea didn't cross my mind, but I would never . . . at least, I don't think I would ever try such a thing."

She smiled. "I'm glad for that."

Remembering what my mother had told me, I searched the woman's face. "Is it true? Is it true what my mother said?"

Anna looked at me questioningly.

"That-that you were—"

She bit her lower lip and nodded. "And there isn't a night goes by but that I remember. Besides a chain-link fence circling my land, I have six locks on every door and wrought-iron filigree on every window. I keep a Scottie dog in the house and two Dobermans that run free on my property."

She took a deep breath. "People will try to tell you that, in time, you'll forget. That's not true. However, you will find ways to deal with your memories. And you will get to where you think of it less and less." She fidgeted with the corner of my bedspread for a moment. "Believe it or not, the sun will shine again. While you'll never trust as you once did, you will give your trust to those who earn it."

I finished the gelatin and handed her the spoon. She placed it and the empty bowl on the stand next to my bed.

"At least you didn't have to deal with the terrible guilt I feel for having caused the rape."

"Oh, really? Heather, believe it or not, every female who's ever been raped, whether four or ninety-four, blames herself. I don't know why this unreasonable guilt always accompanies rape, but it does." Anna nibbled on her lower lip, then continued. "In my case, the two boys came to my door. They said their car broke down, and they needed to call a repairman. Stupidly, I invited them into my home." Her face paled; her eyes glassed over. I imagined she was reliving the crime in her mind. "They stole more than my television and my VCR. They stole my peace of mind."

"I-I-I'm sorry. How could God let such a thing happen?"

"It wasn't God's fault. God is a God of love. And in love, He created sons and daughters to be free moral agents, not robots who respond automatically. That means He gave them the freedom of choice, including my assailants. He wants us to love Him willingly. Unfortunately, sometimes humans make bad choices, choices that hurt innocent people."

"But He could stop them, couldn't He? He could have kept Josh from, from—" I couldn't make myself say the word.

"Yes, He could. But if He did, if He prevented people from ever hurting one another, if He stopped every car accident and every plane crash, if He destroyed the Hitlers and the serial killers of this world from carrying out their heinous crimes, He would be going against His own principles of love. He would be removing the power of choice."

"But how can a loving Father just stand there and watch little children be shot and killed or watch while I—" I closed my eyes in pain.

Anna brushed her hand across my forehead. "Sweetheart, I don't have all the answers. I guess there are some things you'll have to wait to ask Him in person."

"But—"

"I do know," she interrupted, "I do know that He promises never to leave me, never to forsake me. So that tells me, if His promises are true, which they are, He suffered right there with me and with you. He endured the humiliation; He feels the pain—"

"A lot of good—"

"And He's giving you the strength to survive, right now, and will continue to do so in the months and years to come." Tenderness filled her eyes. "Oh, honey, the best thing to come out of my ordeal is I came to know Jesus as I'd never known Him before—that, and I found a new purpose to my life, helping women like yourself come through their tragedies as survivors and not as crippled victims." She fluffed my pillow and adjusted the covers around me. "When my husband died ten years ago, I thought I'd outlived my usefulness. I was wrong. Through my tragedy, God gave me a whole new purpose to my life."

I thought about Mrs. Holtzmann's words for some time. I wasn't sure I wanted to worship a God like she described. I'd always been taught that my guardian angel would protect me from all evil. The more I thought about her words, the more questions I had. I vowed I'd study it out for myself once things settled down in my life again.

". . . Through the Valley"

JOSH

The words "a willing spirit to sustain me" played over and over in my mind throughout the lunch my mother made for me and throughout the drive to the courthouse. My attorney met us in the parking lot. As we made our way to the courthouse, I spotted Dr. Madison waiting for me on the courthouse steps. I looked for a way to avoid him but could find none. The man greeted me with a smile and a hug. Nervous, I introduced him to my mother and to Mr. Dodd.

"Josh, could I speak with you for just a minute before we go inside?" Dr. Madison looked first at me, then at my attorney.

The lawyer nodded. "Mrs. West and I will wait for you inside, Joshua."

I cast the attorney a weak smile.

We watched them climb the rest of the steps and enter the courthouse. When they'd gone, Dr. Madison placed his hand on my shoulder. "Josh, Gerrie and I feel terrible about what has happened. During the last three years, you've become like a son to us, the son we never had. Please know that I'm not here to condemn you. I just wanted to let you know that we still love you. And I wanted to pray with you before you went inside, if that's all right."

I swallowed the lump in my throat and bowed my head.

"Dear heavenly Father, be with Josh today as he . . ." Dr. Madison's rich, warm tones washed gently over me. He prayed for me, for the lawyers, for the judge, for Heather, and for her family. ". . . may the Holy Spirit fill the courtroom and take control of everyone present. Amen."

At the mention of Heather, my heart leapt. I barely heard the rest of his prayer. The instant we opened our eyes, I grabbed his wrist. "Have you talked with Heather? How is she? Is she all right?"

"No, she refused to see anyone from the college. Her mother suggested that we wait a few days." His eyes misted over. The anguish in his face wrenched at my heart. "Oh, Joshua, I won't lie to you. Mrs. MacKenna says Heather's hurting badly. I am told that she attempted to commit suicide." He cleared his throat. "It's going to take her a long time to heal."

Suicide? I closed my eyes and ran my fingers through my hair. "I'm so sorry, Dr. Madison, for what I've done. And I'm so sorry for disappointing you."

"Joshua." He glanced toward the doors at the top of the steps. "Your lawyer is motioning for you. You'd better go. We'll talk later."

"Are you coming in?"

He shook his head. "No, I don't think so." Dr. Madison turned and jogged down the steps. I watched until he disappeared around the corner of the courthouse. With leaden feet, I climbed the rest of the steps and entered the building.

Up until I learned of Mac's attempted suicide, my male pride wanted to deny having raped her, while my conscience hammered away at my guilt. The full impact of what I'd done hit me when I entered the courtroom. *This is real, very, very real. No TV drama here. No commercial breaks. No rosy conclusion at the end of the hour.*

I glanced over at Heather, hoping to catch her eye. *Suicide? Oh, Mac, I'm so sorry. I had such dreams for us. I never meant for things to end like this.* Heather never looked my way. Her mother and father did, though. Her father's rage accosted me like a wrecking ball. When his wife saw me, her eyes narrowed with disgust. Chris glared as only Chris can do. But what did me in was the expression of disappointment and confusion on the face of Mac's little sister René. *A willing spirit, Lord. Sustain me with a willing spirit.*

Before we had entered the courtroom, my lawyer spelled out all the possibilities that could occur if the case went to trial. I thought I was ready for anything. He'd even warned me that I'd drawn the only female judge in the county—Judge Diaz. "She's gonna be tough on you, Josh. But Judge Diaz is known to always be fair."

I smiled. It really didn't matter, now that I could admit my guilt to myself. I'd committed the crime, and I was ready to take whatever consequences might be in store for me. In my desire to erase my guilt, I told Mr. Dodd to change my plea from not guilty to guilty. I was trying to explain this to Mr. Dodd when the judge entered the courtroom. My attorney signaled for me to be silent.

As Judge Diaz read through the counts of assault and rape being brought against me, it was as if she were talking about someone else. Suddenly I felt a jab in my side. Startled, I looked first at Mr. Dodd, then at the judge.

Judge Diaz leaned across the bench. "I asked you, Mr. Hanson, how do you plead?"

Mr. Dodd and I stood to our feet. Mr. Dodd spoke. "Your Honor, my client pleads—"

"Ma'am?" Mr. Dodd paused and looked across the aisle at the assistant district attorney. "Ma'am, I'd like to request a short recess."

The judge frowned. "Will the counsels for the plaintiff and the defense please approach the bench?"

Confused, I glanced over at Heather. She sat with hands covering her eyes. Chris and René glared across the courtroom at me with abject hatred in their eyes. Mac's mother and father whispered to her over the dividing bannister. An older woman whom I didn't recognize sat beside Mrs. MacKenna and seemed actively involved in the conversation. When the lawyers walked up to the bench, I glanced around at my mother sitting behind me. *What's happening?*

She shrugged and shook her head. After the lawyers conferred with the judge for a moment, the two men returned to their seats. The judge pounded the gavel, calling the court back to order.

"The assistant district attorney has informed me that the plaintiff has requested that all charges against the defendant be dropped. This will require the district attorney's office to review the evidence and decide whether or not to proceed with the prosecution of Mr. Hanson. Mr. Hanson?"

I scrambled to my feet beside my attorney. "Yes, Your Honor?"

"This is only a temporary reprieve, not an exoneration. Consider yourself still restricted by the terms of your bail. Do you understand?"

"Yes, ma'am."

"Good. Mr. Moore, I will expect notification from your office regarding the district attorney's decision on whether or not to prosecute the charges by noon Wednesday. Is that clear?"

"Yes, ma'am."

Dazed, I allowed my lawyer to lead me from the courtroom into a small anteroom. My mother followed.

"What happened?" she demanded. "What is going on, Mr. Dodd?"

The lawyer shook his head. "From what I understand, Miss MacKenna doesn't want to go through the trauma of a rape trial. She's decided not to press charges."

"Wonderful!" I grinned over at my mom. "Isn't that great?"

The lawyer rested his hand on my arm. "Hold on there, boy. Remember what the judge said. That doesn't mean it's over for you. Just because she doesn't wish to prosecute doesn't mean the district attorney's office won't."

"But I thought . . ."

"This isn't a civil suit, son. You committed a crime, a crime against Miss MacKenna, hence a crime against the people of this state. While the district attorney's office reviews their evidence and decides whether or not to prosecute, I will be in their faces, trying to convince them to drop the charges. This is where I earn my fee."

While I didn't fully understand the process, I nodded as if I did.

"Joshua." Mr. Dodd moved within inches of my face, nose to nose. "I'm going to talk to you like a Dutch uncle, and I want you to listen to every word I say. Is that clear?"

I nodded.

"What you did was wrong, regardless of the D.A.'s decision not to prosecute. I think you know that now."

Nodding, I stared down at my hands. "I lost my head for a moment. It was wrong, I know that now. But lust is lust, I guess."

"Hold up there!" The man grabbed my chin, forcing me to look him in the eye. "I've defended a number of rape cases, everything from incest to gang rape. Rape is a crime of violence, not of passion or lust. Violence! Did you hear me, son?" The lawyer poked his finger into my chest to accent every word. "Somewhere inside you, Joshua, is a fierce anger. If you don't find a healthy way to deal with that anger, it will erupt again, perhaps in the same way or perhaps in an even more violent way." Now he had my attention.

Mr. Dodd then turned to my mother. "Mrs. West, if the district attorney's office drops the charges, and I'm hopeful that they will—rape cases are the most difficult to prove in a courtroom, even in this day and age—if you want my advice, take your son back to California with you and take him to a good therapist. Joshua's very, very angry at something. The quicker he finds out what it is, the better it will be for him and for everyone around him."

"Sir." I nibbled on my lower lip. "Can I speak with Heather, alone, for a few minutes? I want to—"

"Oh-ho-ho-ho, no!"

"How about a letter? I could write her a letter."

The lawyer shook his head emphatically. "The stupidest thing you could do right now would be to try to contact her in any way, shape, or form. The best advice I can give you—and you are paying for my advice, remember, so listen—is this: from this moment on, forget Heather MacKenna; never try to see her or contact her again; erase her from your memory; run as far away from her as possible. Get a fresh start around people who don't know what you've done."

Leave school? My mouth dropped open. "But I'm starting my senior year here. All my friends—"

He placed his hand on my arm. "Trust me on this, Josh; attend a college in California or Florida or Johannesburg,

South Africa, for that matter. Just get away from here. And, please, get professional help as soon as possible. That needs to come first."

I thought about Mr. Dodd's advice as we left the court-house. At the far end of the parking lot, I thought I saw Heather and her parents getting into their car, but I wasn't sure. It was too far away. My mother must have seen them also, for she grabbed my arm. "Come on, Josh, let's go back to your apartment and decide what to do next."

I nodded and followed her to my car.

Chapter Seven:

"A Rainbow . . ."

HEATHER

After a long talk with Dr. Walters, she released me from the hospital into my parents' care. "Remember your appointment tomorrow morning at the outpatient clinic for the rest of your tests," she called as the nurse helped me into a wheelchair and adjusted the footrests.

I laughed and assured her I would be there. "If you knew my mother's compulsion for meeting appointments on time, you wouldn't worry."

"Speaking of your mother, you should know that Mrs. Holtzmann talked with your parents about the attack. She wanted to pave the way for you."

I smiled weakly. "I know."

The doctor nodded. "Anna's a good woman. Just remember we're all on your side, rooting for you."

Tears filled my eyes. I tried to smile. "I know. And I'm grateful."

Dr. Walters gestured for the nurse to take me to my parents' waiting car.

The familiar smell and feel of my dad's Pontiac immediately enveloped me like a protective cocoon. My father drove without saying a word. Every once in a while, he'd glance over at me, swallow hard, then return his attention to his driving. When he passed the motel where Chris and I had stayed, I pointed. "Daddy, you missed the turn."

"Your mother and I decided to move you to a motel up the street. It's a little better quality, plus they had a suite of rooms available. Dr. Walters suggested that we stay close to you at all times during the next few days. And the suite . . ." His voice dropped to a mumble.

I nodded. *They all think I've gone psycho! Maybe they're right. Maybe I have.*

"Your mother stayed in the suite with your sister while I came to pick you up. René's pretty upset by everything that's happened."

And it's all my fault. "I'm sorry." Inside, I withered a little more.

"It's OK, princess. You just concentrate on your feeling better. René's going to be fine too, I promise. Oh, by the way, Mrs. Peters, the women's dean, called. She and the college president's wife wanted to visit you in the hospital, but Mama suggested they wait a while."

Hooray for Mama! "I appreciate that."

My father continued. "Knowing you must be hungry and might not feel up to going out to a restaurant, your mother ordered a pizza and soda for us all. You do like pizza, don't you?"

"Of course, Daddy." I smiled to myself. *I haven't changed that much.* I touched the side of my face. *Oh, no, my jaw.*

We passed the street where Josh lived. "Have you seen Josh?"

My father's face tensed. His grip on the steering wheel turned his knuckles white. "No! And for his sake, I had better not! I'm glad you finally came to your senses and filed charges against that—"

"But I—" The unsaid words hung in the air between us. I sank lower in the seat. I glanced over at him out of the corner of my eye.

He took two deep breaths before he spoke again. "You have an appointment with the assistant district attorney tomorrow morning immediately following your medical appointment."

"Oh, no!" I whimpered. "I can't do it, Daddy. I can't go

through the horrid details again." Biting my lip, I turned toward my window.

He eased the car into the motel parking lot. Pulling into the space at the end of building, he braked and turned off the ignition. The end-room door burst open, and René ran to my side of the car.

"Heather! Heather, how are you?" She pulled open the door and threw her arms about my neck. "I am so, so sorry." Tears flowed down her cheeks.

I fumbled to unlatch the seat belt. My father came around the vehicle and helped me into the motel room. I stepped inside the room and into my mother's waiting arms.

During the hours that followed, they ate pizza together while I drank soda pop. We watched TV and laughed at a silly movie on the old-time movie channel. I almost forgot why my folks were there—almost.

On Monday morning, I endured the humiliation of the examination at the hospital and the questions at the district attorney's office. Of the two, the latter was far worse. If I thought Sheriff Hicks gave me the third degree, the assistant district attorney's barrage of questions must have been to the tenth degree.

"Now, Miss MacKenna, I must level with you. Rape cases are difficult to win. It involves long, humiliating interrogations on the witness stand." He eyed me over his horn-rimmed glasses. "The defense lawyer will do everything he can to make you look bad—that's his job. And Mr. Hanson's lawyer, Mr. Dodd, is one of the best criminal attorneys in the county, probably the state. Just so you know what you're up against."

Scenes from television's "L.A. Law" and "Matlock" flashed through my mind. What should I do? I knew that I couldn't survive the kind of abuse he described. It would be like being raped all over again, and this time in public! I glanced over at my mother—she was crying—then at my father. Both avoided looking my way.

"Miss MacKenna, I'm only telling you this so that you have all the facts so you can make an intelligent, well-thought-out decision. This afternoon, at the arraignment, you don't need to say or do anything."

"What will happen?"

The lawyer got into his subject. "Basically, Judge Diaz will review the evidence and either dismiss the charges or hold the case over for trial. However, if you have any ideas of dismissing the charges against this young man, as a favor to me, please do it before we reach the trial stage." He ran his hands through his thinning hair. "I have a stack of litigation that would choke a Supreme Court judge."

My father, who'd been silent during the entire interview, lunged toward the attorney's desk, his face red with anger. "Mr. Moore, look at her black eye. Look at the bruises on her neck. They match the ones crisscrossing her body. How can you sit there and advise my daughter to let that horny creep go free?"

The man shook his head. "Sir, I'm not suggesting that at all. For that matter, we have a strong case against Mr. Hanson, stronger than many. I just want your daughter to know what she's up against in the courtroom and in the media."

Terror shot through me. "Media? What media? I-I don't want any of my friends to know what happened. Oh, dear God, no! Isn't there some way to keep all of this quiet, maybe request a closed courtroom or something?"

The man tapped his fingers impatiently on the desktop. "I hate to tell you this, Miss MacKenna, but your story made front-page news Friday morning. And there will be reporters in the courtroom today."

"Did they use my name?" I screeched.

"You are of age. They have a perfect right. It's called the First Amendment to the Constitution."

My father stormed to the window. "So you're saying I should pack up my daughter and steal away into the night?"

"No, not at all. Sir, please try to understand the situation." The attorney closed his eyes and rubbed his forehead. "The National Victims' Center in Arlington, Virginia, reports that of the more than seven hundred thousand women raped in America last year, only twenty-two percent of those rapes were committed by strangers. The other seventy-eight percent of the perpetrators are either family members, casual acquaintances, or, as in your daughter's case, boyfriends. And, for obvious reasons, the most difficult to prove are the date rapes."

I closed my eyes and tried to block out the assistant D.A.'s words but failed. "Date or acquaintance rape isn't a wild stranger jumping out of a bush and attacking you. The circumstances are more subtle. Jurors struggle with the notion that some young women invent rape charges to assuage their guilty consciences for indulging in sex before marriage, especially if there was consensual kissing or fondling involved."

My eyes flew open. I cried out, "I admit that I let him kiss me, but that's all. I tried to make him stop. I really tried." I buried my face in my hands.

My mother drew me into her arms and comforted me while my father glared at my accuser from across the room. Mr. Moore reached out his hand toward me. "Miss MacKenna, I didn't say you did. I'm just telling you what you're up against."

Walking behind my chair, my father placed his hand on my shoulder and squeezed it gently. "So, what do you recommend?"

The lawyer took a deep breath. "I recommend that you go for a ride in your car and talk it over as a family, since your decision involves the entire family. But, remember, the final decision must be yours, Heather. And whatever you decide, I'll meet you on the steps of the courthouse at one-forty-five for the two-o'clock arraignment."

"That's it? That's all there is?" My mother stormed from the building ahead of my father and me. "Justice. They call this justice?"

We climbed into the car and drove through the countryside, past long rows of immature stalks of corn. My father ranted, and I listened. My mother harangued, and I listened. All the while I remembered Mrs. Holtzmann's words. *At any time, you can change your mind. It's up to you, Heather—no one else!*

Taking two deep breaths, I stifled the urge to scream.

"Daddy, can you take me to see Mrs. Holtzmann?" I measured my tone of voice carefully. "If anyone understands my situation, she does."

My mother whirled around in the seat to face me. "Heather, your father and I are trying very hard to understand how you feel."

"I know that, Mama. And I thank you for all you are doing, but I need to talk with Mrs. Holtzmann."

"Fine!" My mother whirled about and stared out the windshield. "Arthur, take Heather to see Mrs. Holtzmann. Maybe the woman can talk some sense into her head."

When we arrived at Anna's place, I suggested that my family go eat lunch and return in time to take me to the courthouse. I spent the next hour with Anna. I wept out of fear of the future. I shouted over the pressure my parents had applied. I raged at Josh. I ranted at the assistant district attorney. All the while, the woman said nothing. When I collapsed on her sofa, her little Scottie dog hopped up onto my lap and licked my face.

"Burnsy hates to see anyone cry," Anna explained. "You rest for a moment while I tell you a few facts about rape. First, as you know, rape shatters a woman's self-esteem. Often, she feels unworthy to even ask for help. As I told you before, nearly seven out of ten women feel responsible. Many wait several hours before reporting the crime, hoping they can solve the problem themselves."

"I wouldn't have told anyone except that Chris insisted I check into the hospital."

Anna sat down beside me and took my hands in hers. "Heather, the facts are that only thirty percent of reported rapes result in arrests. Of those, only about twelve percent ever go to court. Either charges are dropped, or there is insufficient evidence to prosecute." She paused to let her words sink in. "Once in court, jurors must be convinced beyond a doubt that force was involved. I don't think it will be difficult to prove that in your case. That's the down side.

"On the up side, almost sixty percent of the women who go to trial see their assailants found guilty. But again, on the down side, thirteen percent of the men convicted are released on probation. And those who go to jail are likely to be back on the streets in less than six years."

"Six years?" I stroked the dog's head.

"Worse yet, statistics tell us that five out of ten of those men will be rearrested for rape within three years of completing their first sentence." She hurried on. "More important than any court trial, any conviction, any prison sentence is you and your well-being. That should be your first priority." She took my hands in hers. "While you've been victimized by rape, you mustn't ever become a victim in here." She pointed to my head. "You are a survivor, Heather, one tough survivor. Always remember that."

A horn honked outside Anna's chain-link gate. She peered out the window. " It's your folks. If we're going to make it to the courthouse by one-forty-five, we need to leave now."

I looked up in surprise. "Wait! What shall I do?"

"You'll know when the time comes." She bustled to the hall closet and grabbed her coat. "Come on; let's not keep the judge waiting."

I stood up and shrugged on my jacket. "You mean you'll go with me?"

She looked at me and smiled. "That's my job, isn't it, to be there for you as long as you need me?"

We hurried out to the car and hopped into the back seat. I could tell that my mother resented Anna's presence.

My father eyed me through the rearview mirror. "So, what did you decide?"

I gulped. "I didn't."

"Didn't what?"

"I didn't decide."

He glared at the road ahead. At the courthouse, Mr. Moore whisked me and my family past a small group of reporters waiting on the steps and into the courtroom. A number of faculty and students filled the rows behind the prosecutor's table. Chris and René came into the courtroom and sat in the row behind my parents. Mrs. Holtzmann arranged to sit directly behind me. My mother's displeasure showed in every line of her body.

Back and forth, my mind swayed. *Prosecute—don't prosecute. Prosecute—don't prosecute.* I'd just about decided not to prosecute when Josh and his attorney entered the courtroom. He caught my eye and smiled. I looked away. *How dare you smile at me as if nothing happened! When I get done with you, we'll see how much you feel like smiling, you, you—Oh, God, what am I saying?*

The bailiff announced the judge's arrival. We all stood, then sat back down. During the judge's opening remarks, the terror started. It began like a chill in the back of my neck and traveled the length of my spine, then spread through my arms and legs. I trembled uncontrollably. *I can't go through with this. I just can't! But if I don't, Mama and Daddy will be furious. My friends will think I lied, then chickened out.* I remembered Anna's words. *Do what's best for me. I've got to do what's best for me, no matter what!*

I grabbed my attorney's sleeve. "I can't do this, Mr. Moore. Please stop the proceedings any way you can."

The lawyer narrowed his eyes. "Are you sure? Are you very, very sure?"

I nodded. By now, my whole body trembled. I looked at Josh's profile. *I hate you, Joshua Hanson, more than you can ever know. If I had my way, I'd see you burn in hell for what you did to me. But I can't go through the humiliation of a trial.* I glanced toward my father. He looked at me curiously. *Sorry, Daddy, but I just can't do this, even for you.*

My parents and I never discussed my decision. On the way home, I tried to tell them why I changed my mind, but they changed the subject. I spent the summer scooping ice cream into cones at an ice-cream shop. I corresponded with Anna and Chris every week. Chris and I promised to exchange visits during the summer.

In June, I made the mistake of writing to Sara, another of my college friends. Of course, I didn't refer to the reason I left school so abruptly. I didn't need to. A week later, Sara's reply arrived. My mother handed me the letter when I got home from work. Delighted, I dashed up to my room and closed the door. I'd been so isolated and alone since coming home from school. Mom and Dad found it awkward to talk with me or even to listen. And René, well, she's my little sister. I didn't want to distort or scar her opinion of men as mine had been.

Eagerly, I tore open the envelope and read the enclosed letter.

Dear Heather,

I was surprised to receive your letter. I admit, I don't exactly know what to say to you. Look, can I be honest with you? I don't understand what's going on. How could you do such a thing to Josh? Totally ruin a guy's life. I thought you were a better Christian than that. He left school. He had to leave after what you did! A man who would have made a terrific preacher for the Lord! You ruined him. How could you?

Some kids here think you made up the whole rape story just to get attention. Was Josh going to dump you or something? Jenny Renfro is telling everyone that Josh was seeing her on the side the whole time the two of you were dating. Is that why you dragged both him and the school through the mud? For revenge?

I crumpled the letter in my hand and threw myself on my bed. *How could Sara think such a thing? Talk about being Christian! How did I turn out to be the villain in this? Aren't Christians supposed to love one another, be there for each other? Doesn't the Bible say, "Judge not that ye be not judged"?*

Later that night I called Chris. At first she told me that Sara's attitude was an isolated reaction. But the more we talked, the more I realized I was not only the hot topic at graduation but in many students' and even a few faculty members' minds, I was the villain. I'd wondered why so few of my friends and teachers had bothered to send a card or letter after I left school.

God, why is this happening to me? Aren't these Your children? How can they be so hateful? Can't You stop them?

But then, why should You? You didn't stop Josh from doing what he did to me, did You?

The thought that God might be to blame for my pain stunned me. Yet to my battered mind, it made sense. I stopped going to church with my parents. After all, how could I be sure that the people I'd known all my life weren't gossiping about me, judging me also? I stuffed my Bible into the bottom drawer of my dresser.

My behavior deteriorated into sudden mood swings, temper outbursts, and irrational panic. Then, for no apparent reason, my anger passed. My tears dried; I felt like a broken toy. I moved like a robot through my days. I felt numb and vacant. And at night? The nightmares I'd had since the rape took on a more sinister nature. Now, not only did Josh tear the clothes from my body, but the faces of those I trusted to be my friends stood around the bed, laughing and cheering him on. Two or three times a night, I awoke sobbing, shaking, and in a drenching sweat. Then with dawn, my senseless, emotionless existence would begin again, interrupted with an exhaustless list of "if onlys." *If only I hadn't stayed in the apartment alone with Josh; if only I'd gotten out of the relationship when I first noticed his anger; if only I'd never gone away to college—if only, if only, if only!*

The repeating nightmares forced me to make an appointment to see a Christian therapist in the area, Dr. Mitchell Ross. Like a beloved grandpa or jolly St. Nicholas, the gentle old man with a thick mane of white hair and mustache to match exuded an air of security. Each week, I looked forward to escaping from my chloroformed world to his office, where I could say whatever I liked. He helped me unleash my anger and my guilt.

Most of the time, I left his office encouraged. But after one particularly difficult session, I returned home to an empty house. I'd reached the breaking point. Suddenly I knew that I couldn't go on anymore. Once people accused me of trying to take my life; now, I'd actually do it. Death would be a welcome visitor. The way I was messing up everyone's lives, it would be the kindest thing I could do. *I'll take pills. Neat, efficient pills. I'll just fall asleep and not wake up. Sleep, without the nightmare, without the pain* . . . I climbed the stairs to the upstairs bathroom. I reached for the handle on the medicine-cabinet door and caught my reflection in the mirror. For the first time in weeks, I really looked at myself in a mirror. Dark rings circled my eyes. My usually peachy complexion appeared jaundiced and gray. My hair draped lifelessly around my face and shoulders. I'd lost so much weight that my clothes hung limp from my shoulders.

I stared at the stranger before me. *Who are you? Why have you taken over my life?* I touched my hand to my face. My skin felt like leather dried by the sun. Like a cancer patient, I was dying from the inside out. Snatching my hand back from the medicine chest knob, I ran to my room, crawled into bed, and sobbed for my lost life. I told no one how close I'd come to the brink of suicide, no one but Dr. Ross.

By fall, Dr. Ross convinced me to take a few classes at the local community college. Instead, I enrolled full time in the university's elementary-teacher-training program. I graduated three years later with my teaching credentials. Dr. Ross held my hand all the way.

Dr. Ross didn't approve of Bill right from the start. The day I arrived at his office with my broken heart in my hands, he listened. A couple years after my fiasco romance with Bill I decided, with Dr. Ross's help, that it was time to break out on my own. I applied for and landed a job at an all-girls' school in Hartford, Connecticut. Dr. Ross referred me to a therapist in Hartford, a Dr. Zigler.

On my last visit to Dr. Ross's office, I thanked him for all the help he'd been during the three years I'd been seeing him. "I couldn't have made it without you, you know."

He arose from his desk, came around to where I stood, and clasped my hands in his. "Heather, my dear, don't sell yourself or your God short. I could only guide you. You and God did the healing work."

"Not God. No, not God." I tried to argue, but he shook his head.

"In time, you'll be able to see traces of His care in your life,

I promise. But beyond that, from the first, I told you that you are much stronger than you think. And I'm proud of you."

My eyes misted. "It still hurts, you know."

"And it always will. Scar tissue is like that, you know." He frowned.

"Will I ever be the same carefree girl again?"

His eyes saddened. "No, I'm afraid not. We can never regain lost innocence." His eyes brightened. "But that's not all bad. You're older, wiser, and stronger for what you've endured. You've learned a lot about yourself. You've not just survived your tragedy, you've been victorious over it."

"Thank you, Dr. Ross." I planted a kiss on his grizzled cheek.

He grinned and gave my hands a squeeze. "Send me an invitation to your wedding, you hear? And a birth announcement for your first child."

I scowled. "I don't see either in my future."

His eyes twinkled as he released my hands. "Heather, Heather, Heather! There's a man out there who's smart enough to know a good thing when he sees it and determined enough to break through your minefield of defenses."

"I know." I giggled. "But, Dr. Ross, it's too late. You're already married, remember?"

He blushed and patted my hand. "Ah, me gel, you do an old man's heart good. I'm going to miss you. When you're around, I feel twenty years younger." He laughed. "Then, of course, I'd still be old enough to be your father."

"I don't care," I protested. "They just don't make gentlemen like they used to. Take it from a woman on the front lines of battle, men like you and my father just don't exist anymore!"

"Remember, child, when your head can't give you the answer, trust your heart." He chuckled and patted my hands again. "Don't make any predictions today. You never know. Life is full of little surprises."

Dr. Ross was right. I was in Hartford a little over a year when an affectionate, easygoing, graduate psych major named Tony moved into the apartment upstairs. By that time I'd begun attending church again and was surprised to learn

Tony belonged to the same one as I.

Poor Tony, I put him through the minefield Dr. Ross predicted. While I didn't follow up on the therapist Dr. Ross suggested, I did find a Christian counselor I could trust during that time. If I hadn't, I don't think Tony and I would have made it past the first six months of our courtship. Most of the credit must go to Tony.

Now, I stared out over the valley and contemplated the biggest decision of my life—marrying Tony. *Maybe it would help if I made an appointment to see Dr. Ross. I need him to tell me if I'm making a mistake or not.* You see, my virginity and my sense of security weren't the only casualties of the rape. Perhaps a greater casualty had been my loss of self-confidence, of being able trust myself to make sound judgments.

I pictured the old man in my mind. *You wouldn't tell me anyway if I'm making a mistake, would you, Dr. Ross? All you'd say is, "If your head can't give you the answer, trust your heart."*

Trust your heart . . .

Tony's loving face surfaced in my mind. I saw his rakish grin, his teasing eyes, his compassionate demeanor. As I gazed out over the valley of golds, oranges, and browns, a peaceful confidence filled me. For the first time in what seemed like a lifetime, I wasn't a rape victim, paralyzed by fear. Instead, I knew my feelings echoed any woman's as she anticipates her wedding day—nervous about her own readiness but confident in the love of her intended.

I thought of my mother and father back home, worrying about me, praying for me. It was about time we sat down and talked together. I thought of René, a little girl robbed of her naiveté before her time. When did she become so wise? But most of all, I thought of Tony. *Tony! Oh, no!* I glanced at my watch. *Oh, no! He'll be calling within the hour. I gotta get home!*

Tossing the car keys into the air, then catching them, I hopped off the boulder and dashed for my car. The last thing I wanted was for him to worry. I could hardly wait to tell him . . . *Tell him? Tell him what?* I laughed because I had no idea what I wanted to tell him. All I knew was, for the first time, I felt free, truly free to say, "I love you"—no strings attached!

The next three weeks disappeared in a flurry of bridal showers, shopping trips, and late-night gab sessions. On my wedding day, clear blue skies and Indian-summer temperatures greeted me. As I slipped the "too-white" gown over my shoulders and waited while my mother fastened each of the tiny satin buttons up the back, I gazed in the three-way mirror at the radiant bride I'd always imagined I'd be. As I watched my best friend and maid of honor Chris twirl my tangle of red locks into manageable curls cascading down my back, I sensed a peace in the eyes of the woman staring back at me in the mirror. As my mother pinned the crown of pearls in place, I noted the blush in my cheeks, not from shame or remorse, but from eager anticipation.

My father escorted me down the aisle. A twinge of fear coursed through me as he withdrew my hand from his protective arm and placed it on Tony's. I took a deep breath and repeated Dr. Ross's advice over and over in my head. *"Trust your heart."*

The music, the flowers, the minister's admonitions blurred through my consciousness. I snapped alert when I heard the words "I now pronounce you husband and wife. You may kiss the bride."

My breath caught in my throat. I turned and gazed into Tony's loving eyes. My eyes filled with tears. *Yes, Lord. Thank You for bringing this incredibly beautiful man into my life. Thank You for bringing something good and wholesome and lovely out of my despair.*

After the prayer, Tony and I turned to face our families and friends. I saw all the people who stood by me, who believed in me—Mama and Daddy, Grandma and Grandpa, René, Chris. I smiled at Mrs. Holtzmann and winked at Dr. and Mrs. Ross. Before I realized what was happening, the minister introduced us as husband and wife, and the organist struck the introductory chord to "Trumpet Voluntary." Tony squeezed my hand. I breathed deeply, then took the first confident step forward as Mrs. Anthony Callente.

" After the Rain"

JOSH

Waiting. I've never been good at waiting. Mr. Dodd told us that he had no idea how long it would take the district attorney's office to review my case. My mother and I drove back to my apartment. As I pulled to a stop in front of my place, my mother gasped. "Oh, dear God . . ."

Garbage lay strewn about my front lawn. Across my door and picture window, someone had spray-painted the words "Rapist, you'll get yours!"

"What the—" I got out of the car and walked up the front walk, picking up rotten vegetables and crumpled news-papers. "Who would do such a thing?"

As we stood gazing on the scene, a car filled with teenage guys drove by, screaming obscenities and throwing raw eggs. I didn't recognize either the boys or their vehicle. One of the eggs hit my chest and splattered. I stared as the yellow yolk slid down the front of my shirt and onto my pants. When I started in the direction they'd gone, my mother grabbed my arm. "Come on, son. Let's go inside and leave this mess until later."

Once the door closed behind us, Mom closed the front drapes while I took the trash I'd collected and put it in the kitchen garbage can. I dabbed at the egg on my shirt and pants with a wet dishcloth. My mother came into the kitchen and examined the stain. "Go change your clothes, and I'll see what I can do about this mess."

I obeyed without a word. What could I say? What was there to say? I deserved what I got. My mother, however, did not. When I returned with the shirt and pants, the telephone rang. I looked at my mother and she, at me. Neither of us moved to answer it. My answering machine clicked in after the third ring. I listened to my voice instruct the caller to leave a message after the beep, then held my breath when the beep sounded. The voice was familiar.

"Hi, Josh? This is Carl. Just wanted to call and see if you were home yet. Hey, man, I don't know what to say, except that I'm with—"

I grabbed the receiver. "Carl? This is Josh."

The voice on the other end of the line suddenly seemed strained. "Hey, glad I caught you, man. I just wanted to know if you're alone, if you need someone to talk to or something . . ."

Tears came to my eyes. I cleared my throat. "Oh, I'm glad you did." I couldn't believe it. I couldn't think of anything to say to Carl, my best friend.

"I suppose the last few days have been rough, huh?"

"Rough hardly describes it."

He paused as if searching for words also. "I heard that Mac dropped the charges."

"Yeah." I studied some dirt under my thumbnail.

"So you're off the hook?"

"Not really. The district attorney's office needs to decide if they want to bring it to trial."

Another pause. "Tough break, man. When will you know?"

I took a deep breath. "Probably by the end of the week, at least I hope so. I can't wait to get out of here."

"You're leaving school?"

I laughed. "Don't act so surprised. What would you do, stay around and be the focus of suspicion and gossip?"

"Naw, I see what you mean. Hey, I sure want to see you before you head west, man. Give me a call, OK?"

I nodded. "Right."

"Look, let's keep in touch."

I heard the hesitation in his voice, the element of false enthusiasm.

"You got it."

We said our goodbyes, and I hung up. That's when I noticed the blinking light on my answering machine. My mother and I exchanged wary glances. I took a deep breath and tapped the replay button. There were seven messages—none worth hearing. After the fourth, I unplugged the machine.

My mother and I didn't speak much the rest of the day. Together we cleaned up the front yard and tried to scrub the paint from the door and window. There were no more incidents. There didn't need to be. I longed to leave the school and never return. That night as I lay awake on the couch, staring into the darkness, I castigated myself for my crime. *Why? Why? Why?*

I thought of Mr. Dodd's words. "Rape is a crime of rage, not passion or lust." *Oh, I'd been angry at Mac, all right. Angry enough to throttle her little*—I sat straight up. My thoughts terrified me. *Rape? Murder? Could I ever be so angry that I could kill?* Before Thursday night, I would have said, "No way!" But after all that had happened, I no longer knew for sure. *If my rage made me lose control enough to rape a woman, couldn't that same rage lead me to take a life?*

A chill swept through my body. I shivered and fell to my knees. "Oh, God," I wailed. "I can't take this anymore. My guilt is strangling the life out of me. Please forgive my heinous sin. Please, take it all away!" I remained on my knees, waiting for God to lift the burden of my crime from me. I begged. I pleaded, but felt no relief. I collapsed, face down, on the floor. *I must find peace. Oh, Lord, I must find peace!* I fell asleep prostrate on the living-room floor.

During the rest of the week, I didn't dress, I didn't shave, I didn't eat, I didn't leave the apartment. While I watched talk show after talk show, Mom collected the necessary packing boxes from the grocery stores around town and packed up my belongings. Personally, I didn't care if she set a match to everything I owned. She took care of the business of signing me out of the college and of subletting my apartment.

The only response she got from me was when she told me she'd found a buyer for my Grand Am. "No! You can't sell my car."

"Don't get excited, Josh. The buyer is willing to wait until everything is settled."

"Mom, I love that car!"

Her eyes filled with tears. "Josh, think about it. If the case is dropped, I wouldn't let you drive across the country alone, not in your condition. We certainly can't afford to have me take off the time to ride with you." She paused, as if afraid to continue. "And if they decide to prosecute, and, well, if . . ."

Friday morning, the district attorney dropped the charges against me. Mr. Dodd said the deciding factor was Heather's decision to return to Pennsylvania. "If she'd been a resident of this state and a cooperative witness, they wouldn't have hesitated to prosecute. You can thank your lucky stars she got cold feet, or you'd probably be spending the next six years in the penitentiary!"

Friday afternoon, I signed over my Grand Am to its new owner, a seventeen-year-old girl with braces, and flew home with my mother to California. The first couple of weeks at home, my mother bugged me about finding a counselor. Everyone she'd suggest, I'd visit once and find something I didn't like. I let my hair and my beard grow, wore faded blue jeans and a grimy T-shirt, and, in general, became totally obnoxious.

She tried to convince me to attend church with her. I laughed. The pastor came to visit. He walked in the front door; I walked out the back. I bought a used Honda with the money from the sale of the Grand Am.

When my mother insisted I help out with the expenses, I got a job slinging burgers at a fast-food place near our house. Girls, booze, and hangovers became my life. When my boss threatened to fire me for missing work, I let up on the booze. But the girls? I couldn't tell you how many I dated during that summer. A different one every night, sometimes two. The only thing that kept me from catching AIDS or some other social disease was I couldn't perform. After the first few attempts, I stopped trying. The fact was, I couldn't get Heather out of my mind.

My mother and I fought incessantly. One night, after coming home drunk, I decided I'd had enough. I packed my clothes and left. I spent a few days with a buddy named Glen and his girlfriend Amy. When I discovered they pushed drugs, I called it quits. Fortunately, I hadn't unpacked. I learned later that the authorities raided the place a couple of days after I left.

I bummed south along the coast, did some surfing in Santa Cruz, got a job pumping gas in Big Sur, and worked as a waiter for a few weeks in Santa Barbara. Restless, I headed for the action at Venice Beach, along with two star-struck teenage girls I picked up along the highway. The three of us crashed in an abandoned shed about a block from the beach. The girls moved on after a couple of weeks, but I stayed. I found a job busing tables in a Chinese restaurant. I liked my boss, and I liked the pay. When Lin Ho, the owner of the restaurant, learned about my living quarters, he invited me to live in a studio apartment over the restaurant in return for my services as an off-hours security guard. There'd been a number of recent break-ins in the area.

The pleasant-faced man and I became friends. One day, he invited me home for dinner, to meet his family. I went. After his very pregnant wife Sela served the food, Lin explained that it was a custom of his family to join hands for the blessing. Feeling awkward, I bowed my head as he prayed.

"Dear Father in heaven, giver of all good things, bless each person in this room. Father, pour out a special blessing on my friend Joshua. Lift his burdens, and give him peace. Amen."

Burdens? Peace? Sweat beaded on my forehead. I opened my eyes, expecting to be the focus of their attention.

"Psst!" Sela signaled to her husband. "You forgot to bless the food."

Lin laughed and blushed. "Oh, yes, and, dear Father, bless the food we are about to eat. May it strengthen us for Your service. Amen."

I laughed nervously, but my hosts seemed unaware of my discomfort. We talked about the restaurant, about the drop in tourists, about the soon arrival of their first child. After the meal, Lin and I took a walk along the beach.

"We're expecting a boy. Sela had to have an ultrasound, so we know ahead of time the child's gender. He will, of course, be named after me, as I was after my father."

"So your son will be Lin Ho the third?"

Lin nodded. "Joshua, I'm curious. Tell me, were you named

after your father?"

"No."

"Then another honored relative perhaps?"

I shook my head. "Not that I know of."

Lin smiled. "Ah, your parents must have named you after the Joshua of the Old Testament. What an honor. Did you know that he was a great leader of his people?"

"Yeah, I know."

Lin flashed a wide, tooth-filled grin. "You are a student of the Bible? How wonderful! I, too, read the Bible." He frowned. "But there is much I don't understand. Would you be willing to teach me? I will pay you."

I cleared my throat. "Well, I don't know if I . . ." *Joshua, the man has given you a place to live. He's given you his friendship. Is he asking so much of you?* "Sure, if you get stuck on anything, I'll try to help, OK?"

"Joshua, you make me so happy. Come on, let's go back to the house and get started."

I closed my eyes for a moment. *What did I get myself into?*

Sensing my hesitation, Lin added, "Will twenty-five dollars an hour be enough? My cousin hired an English tutor for twenty dollars an hour. Surely God's Word is worth more than man's."

I shook my head and gestured. "Forget the money, Lin. You're my friend. I'll be glad to help you any way I can."

I could barely keep up with Lin as he rushed back to his home and told Sela the good news. With pride, Lin brought out two new Bibles. "I bought these, one for Sela and one for me." He handed me Sela's. "Please keep this as yours. My wife and I will share until I can get another at the bookstore tomorrow."

I glanced about the couple's modest home and saw no Far Eastern gods or shrines. "How did you get interested in the Bible?"

Lin smiled. "In Hong Kong, a student from the United States taught Sela and me English. She taught us about God as well. However, it wasn't until I got here to America that I could afford to buy our own Bibles."

When I asked him where he wanted to start reading, Lin beamed with happiness. "With Jesus, of course." Because of the imminent arrival of their child, I suggested we start reading the Gospel of Luke. Lin would read a verse, and we'd discuss it. Then Sela would read a verse. By mutual agreement, we stopped when the first rays of dawn broke over the San Gabriel Mountains.

As I prepared to leave, he shook my hand. "Joshua, my friend, I thank you for sharing your Jesus with us. We'll read more tonight?"

I'm not sure if it was due to sleep deprivation or the Holy Spirit, but I agreed to meet with him and Sela again to study the Bible after the restaurant closed that evening. I said goodbye and walked back to my room over the restaurant.

While I denied that our Bible studies meant anything to me, I soon found myself looking forward to them. My drinking lessened. I didn't have the time or the patience for the resulting hangover.

A brilliant student, Lin kept me on my toes by asking incredibly perceptive questions. The night Sela gave birth to their son, Lin and I walked home from the hospital together. Lin suggested we walk out onto the pier before parting. In the darkness, as we watched the phosphorescent waves lap against the pilings, Lin gave his heart to the Lord. My face reddened. I was speechless. I'd been instrumental in bringing someone to Christ but hadn't found Him myself.

Like the jailer of old, Lin asked, "What must I do to be saved?"

I cleared my throat. "According to Acts 16:31, you must 'believe on the Lord Jesus Christ.' "

"That's all? That's it?" he asked, his voice filled with urgency.

"On the day of Pentecost, Peter told the people to 'repent and be baptized.' "

He leaned his elbows on a piling. "Repent of my sins? I understand that. But how can I know for sure, Joshua, that I've been forgiven?"

Oh, God, I can't do this. You know I can't. I turned to walk back to the beach. He caught my arm. "Please, I've got to know. There . . . there are some less than honorable things in my past. They are why I came to America in the first place."

His words hit me like a slap across the face. *Less than honorable—Lin?* I inhaled deeply. "Lin, you must take God's forgiveness by faith. God promises that 'if we confess our sins, he is faithful and just and will forgive us our sins and purify us from all unrighteousness.' "

"Faith. Just have faith. This is incredible. In the religion of my fathers, I would need to do penance for my sins. But you say that Jesus has already done my penance, on the cross."

"That's about it." I glanced at Lin. A spotlight on a nearby pole illuminated Lin's face. I'd never seen such radiance and joy as I saw on his face that night. In my heart I cried out, *Oh, Lord, if only I could know such joy and peace once again. If only I could accept Your simple promises. If only I could accept You again for the first time . . .*

We hurried back to Lin's living room. He wanted to hear more. He wanted to read for himself the promises of forgiveness. In the middle of reading Hebrews 8, verse 12, Lin stopped and reread the line. "I will forgive their wickedness and will remember their sins no more." He read the verse a third time. "I will forgive their wickedness and will remember their sins no more."

Silently, he stared at the Bible for many seconds. When he lifted his eyes to me, tears streamed down his cheeks. "Josh, before I left home, I did a terrible thing, something so terrible that I was sent from my father's house to avoid arrest and public humiliation." He held his breath for a moment, then continued. "Only my wife and my father know the whole story. If I told you, you would not want to be my friend."

Heather's accusing face flashed before my eyes; my face reddened. "Lin, I've done some stupid things in my life too."

"No, Joshua, not stupid—evil. I allowed my brother to go to prison for something I did. I ran down a bicyclist on my way home from my bachelor's party. Both my brother and I had been drinking."

I lifted my hand to stop him, but Lin waved me away. "My

father didn't want to jeopardize the important union that would be established between Sela's and my families after our wedding. So my older brother, who is yet unmarried, agreed to take the blame." Lin dropped to his knees before me. "Please, Josh, you know this Man Jesus better than I. Please tell me that He can forgive this terrible thing I did!"

I hid my eyes with my hands. *Oh, God, forgive me for doubting You all these years. I've known the truth, yet denied it. Help me to assure my friend of Your loving compassion for the worst of sinners.*

Lin didn't understand my silence. Fear filled his face. "I must know I'm forgiven. Please pray with me."

I swallowed hard. My insides trembled like partially set gelatin. I dried the slick palms of my hands on my jeans.

His prayer was simple, as simple as God's promise of forgiveness. In trusting, childlike terms, he confessed his wrong to God and to me. When he finished his prayer and started to rise, I slid to my knees.

"Father, I am not worthy to call You my Father. I've made such a mess of my life. It wasn't enough to rape Heather and try to destroy my mother with my anger. But I had to sleep in the sties with the pigs and eat their slop." I sighed. "Worst of all, Lord, I denied You. I had the answers. I knew where to go for help, but I rejected You. You forgave David of adultery. You forgave Paul of murder. Can You forgive me too?"

For the first time in years, the heavy burden of guilt lifted from my shoulders. Closer than brothers, we clung to each other. Tears flowed. The world seemed light years away, and heaven, but a step.

I called home the next day and made things right with my mother. We both cried. To be honest, I cried more in twenty-four hours than I had in years. A week later, after putting Lin and his little family in the hands of a local pastor, I bade my friends goodbye and headed home.

The first week, when we attended church together, my mother couldn't contain her joy. She introduced me to everyone, especially the young single women in the congregation. When I told her I wasn't looking for female companionship, she waved my objections away.

However, I knew myself better than she. The rage that drove me to rape Mac still erupted every now and then. Even as a Christian, it took very little to send me into a tantrum. No, a relationship with a woman would have to wait until I had something of value to offer her.

After three long years, I finally took Mr. Dodd's advice and started seeing a Christian psychologist. I liked Dr. Warren the minute I met him. He helped me work through my anger. He helped me see that, for years, I'd blamed my mother for sending my dad away. He helped me rebuild my self-esteem.

When I read an ad in the newspaper for an orderly in one of the local hospitals, I applied for and landed the job. A month on the job, and I knew I'd found my true calling. I wanted to become a physical therapist. I worked a year to save up enough money to go back to school.

During that year, I met Teri, a tall, willowy, green-eyed, flaxen-haired, twenty-four-year-old bundle of energy. She worked in the emergency room as a nurse. We met over a seventy-five-year-old asthma patient. Somehow, in the process of monitoring the old man's breathing, we began to share our dreams. I told her about my dream to return to school to study physical therapy.

"You'll be a good P.T. I can tell that you really care about people."

I grinned. "Thanks. How about you? Do you have any wild dreams or outrageous fantasies?"

She laughed. "As a matter of fact, I do. I'm saving my money to spend a year as a Peace Corps volunteer in Bangladesh."

"Really? I'm impressed." I looked at the vibrant young woman with new respect. "When do you leave?"

"I go to Washington, D.C., for a training course in August."

Teri and I managed to "run into" each other on a regular basis. We took our breaks together. We just happened to arrive at the cafeteria at the same time. Before long, we began seeing each other outside the hospital. With each encounter, I grew more and more attached to Teri.

Knowing she'd be leaving soon for Peace Corps training

and knowing I'd been on my own too long to continue living with my mother, I applied to the University of California at Santa Cruz and was accepted.

I took Teri to dinner at a small Italian restaurant the night before she left. Over pasta primavera, I admitted to her that I hated to see her go. "You will write, won't you?"

She reached across the table and took my hand in hers. "You know I will."

I took her to the airport the next morning. Loneliness blended with a healthy serving of relief as I watched her fly out of my life. *Maybe when you return, maybe if you come back to me, I'll be ready for you, Teri. Maybe . . .*

The weekend before Labor Day, I located a studio apartment in town, got a job as an orderly in a nursing home, and signed up for a full load of classes. Many of the courses I took as a theology major couldn't be transferred. My mother helped me move into the apartment. We scoured the second-hand stores for furniture and kitchen supplies. An ad on a grocery-store bulletin board brought me Nerf. My life settled into a comfortable routine of work, classes, writing to Teri, and running on the beach with Nerf. Occasionally I dated for special events at the church or the university, but never the same girl more than once or twice.

At the end of the first year, Teri signed up for a second term. The news produced a twinge of disappointment. I talked over my reaction with God and decided that was a good sign. Maybe I could learn to feel again. When the time came for Teri to enlist again, I held my breath. She announced her decision to return home in a postscript at the end of a twelve-page letter.

Epilogue

HEATHER

It may seem to others that my story has a happily-ever-after ending and that the love of a good man can make everything right. Nothing is so simple. I had to do a lot of healing before I could begin to recognize a good man when I saw one. I had to become whole within myself, or Tony would have acquired an emotional cripple for a wife instead of a mature woman, capable of giving and receiving love. Yet the ghost of Josh continues to affect our lives today.

Even after all this time, silly things bring back disturbing memories. For instance, I can become unglued when I see a blond male of Josh's height and build walking along the street. I don't sing in public anymore, not even at church, during the congregational singing. And I don't wear sundresses.

With my marriage to Tony, the frequency of the horrid nightmares has diminished. On the nights they do come, he holds me gently in his arms, and together, we ask God to send the peace He promised His children. Tony is helping me see that, for my sake, I must forgive Josh. And it's coming.

I still can't watch a video that depicts violence against women, especially one with rape scenes. I panic if Tony tries to capture me in his arms or hold me against my will, even in play. One time, a few weeks ago, we were crossing a busy street in Hartford when Tony suddenly grabbed me and pressed me to his chest. Not having seen the oncoming van,

I panicked. I kicked, screamed, and pummeled his chest, struggling to break free of his grasp. After the danger passed, I couldn't shake my fears. I cringed each time he touched my arm or reached for my hand.

On the positive side, I've built a new relationship with God. He's no longer a sugar daddy, doling out or withholding the goodies from His little girl. In the book of Job, I found a different God, a God who no longer fit my childish jewelry-box image. And I liked what I found. I realized I can be whole in Him, that my goal is to live out His plan, not to coax Him into fulfilling my plans. I discovered that while He doesn't always override the tragedies in life, He keeps His word. He was right there with me in Josh's bedroom, suffering my humiliation, feeling my pain, never leaving my side. And since that fateful night, He's been with me every step of the way, filling me with His strength, His love, and, finally, His peace.

Then, just when I felt competent to go it alone, just when I felt whole once more, He brought Tony into my life. My gregarious Italiano forced me to reach out to others. He helped me see my pain as a vehicle for touching others who are suffering. Tony and I volunteer an evening a week at the Community Crisis Hot Line. Helping others cope heals me as well. Listening to other women's stories reminds me that healing takes time—years, in fact.

What else have I learned? Oh, the list is endless. I've discovered that if a tragedy doesn't kill you, it makes you stronger. I've learned to identify potentially dangerous situations and to avoid them, when possible. I take careful safety precautions when I am home alone or traveling alone, even on an outing to the grocery store.

Outside of Tony and my dad, I don't trust many men. I know that's not fair. I tell myself that most are kind, respectful, and decent. The problem lies within me, not them. I don't trust myself to be able to tell the difference between the good and the bad.

When I tell my story to teenage girls and women at high schools and church groups, I encourage them to learn how to defend themselves against possible attack, to take classes in self-defense at their local YMCA. I advise every woman to be aware of the danger signals in a poor relationship, to listen to that inner voice—it's usually right. I warn them to always be on the alert and aware of their surroundings. I teach them ways they can plan ahead on what they will do before the threat occurs, so their movements will become automatic.

While my public presentation is calm and matter of fact, privately, I'm furious that we women are forced to live in a constant state of tension and fear. But it is a social condition I cannot change. Maybe that's another lesson I'm learning—change what you can change, improve when you can improve, learn from your mistakes, and protect yourself, as best you can, against everything else.

It's a strain to go back home to Pennsylvania. My parents still treat me like a porcelain doll wrapped in cotton batting. At times, I think they blamed me for my poor judgment with Josh, and at other times, they blamed themselves. And I know that, if I had to do everything over, there are many things I would have done differently. Yet, while I made a series of poor decisions regarding my relationship with Josh, it was still his decision to violate my person—not mine.

Beyond the vain regrets we all harbored, their greatest would be my decision not to prosecute. I'm not sure they ever understood or agreed. But, now, after all these years, I know that it really doesn't matter, since it was my decision to make. While I can't speak for other young women, I've never regretted dropping the charges. I've had close friends tell me that I let womankind down when I failed to make Josh pay for his crime, but I had to do what was best for me. I never wanted to be a hero and certainly not a martyr.

I'm not saying all rapists should go free to rape again. Hardly! If I've learned anything while working with rape victims like myself, each case is different, and each victim is different. What one woman may have the strength to endure would crush another under the strain. After saying that, I must add that I am amazed again and again at the resiliency of the human spirit and the power of a loving God to heal even the most tragic wounds.

JOSHUA

Teri will be home for Christmas. A part of me aches to see her again, another part of me quakes under the prospect. She doesn't know about Heather. That's why, when Heather's wedding announcement arrived yesterday with René's note tucked inside, I panicked. Come Christmas, I can no longer avoid the inevitable. She must be told. That tragedy shaped whom I've become.

If the Lord brings us together, as He seems to be doing, I will be a much different husband than I would have been had the rape never occurred. I know I owe it to her to tell her about Mac. And I owe it to our relationship. I'm afraid she'll hate me for what I did. I'm not sure how much I should tell her. Yet she needs to know. Most of all, I don't want to hurt her.

Looking at René MacKenna's bitter note, I am reminded again of what Mr. Dodd said the day he told me of the D.A.'s decision not to prosecute. Thrilled with the news, I looked at my mom and grinned. "The nightmare is finally over!"

Before I finished my sentence, Mr. Dodd pointed his finger at me. "Trust me, Joshua, your nightmare will not be over for a long, long time. Rape is a crime in which everybody loses—the victim, the perpetrator, and their families. And, yes, even future loved ones will be haunted by the memory."

That day, I could never have imagined just how right the attorney would prove to be. Yet, for all my pain, there has been victory. Praise God! He forgives the vilest of sins and the vilest of sinners. He forgave me. Perhaps He can help Teri do the same.

The Facts on Acquaintance Rape

Rape. Mere mention of the word is enough to scare any female. When most women think of a rapist, they picture a stranger leaping out of the bushes at them as they walk by. What they don't realize is that in four out of five rapes, the victim knows her attacker. Rape is a serious crime. The consequences can be devastating for the victim and her family. It should be noted that while men are sometimes the victim of rape, the numbers are so low that they were not figured into the following statistics:

● One in four women will be raped in her lifetime. Those at highest risk are between the ages of fifteen and twenty-four.
● The largest percentage of rapists are white (59.2 percent). Black men constitute 26.2 percent of rapists. Forty percent of all rapists are between the ages of twenty-one and twenty-nine.
● The average sentence of a convicted rapist in the U.S., according to data collected by the Bureau of Justice Statistics, is seven years.
● Only 16 percent of the rapes committed are reported to the police.
(Source: 1992 National Women's Study, a government-financed, independently conducted survey of four thousand women over three years' time.)

What can a woman do? While there is no guaranteed formula for preventing sexual assault, a woman can improve her chances by practicing the following prevention strategies.

On a Date:

1. Trust your instincts. If something doesn't "feel" right, it probably isn't.

2. Be assertive and honest. Avoid playing coy or helpless. Don't play games.

3. Communicate your expectations to one another. Send consistent signals. If he makes unwanted advances, communicate loud and clear to him. Get angry or hostile. Hesitating can send him the wrong message.

4. Double-date until you get to know him.

5. If you live alone, offer to meet him somewhere. If you feel uncomfortable, call a friend to come and get you.

6. Avoid being alone with him at his place. Most date rapes occur in male places of residence.

7. Alcohol is often involved in date rape. Plan your dates without it.

8. Spend time getting to know one another as friends.

    a. Watch for signals of violence and unwarranted fits of anger. Does he demand to have his way? Or lose his cool whenever crossed?

    b. Beware if he attempts to make you feel guilty or accuses you of being "uptight." When things go wrong, is it always someone else's fault?

    c. Be concerned if he acts excessively jealous or possessive.

    d. Seriously question the relationship if he comes on strong sexually from the beginning.

    e. Beware of a man who ignores your wishes.

    f. Never make excuses for unacceptable behavior (i.e., drinking, tantrums, uncontrollable rage, bouts of depression).

9. Carry emergency phone money with you.

10. Tell a friend or family member where you are going and

when you expect to return home.

In General:

1. Be aware of your surroundings at all times, inside and outside of buildings.

2. Avoid isolated areas.

3. Trust your instincts. If you feel threatened, scream and run for the nearest area populated with other people.

4. Learn self-defense techniques by enrolling in a class. Do you know how to kick or hit someone effectively when being attacked? Do you know how to break free when someone grabs you? Learn what everyday objects you could use to defend yourself.

5. Always lock your car, whether inside or out. When going to your car, have your keys in your hand, ready to use as a weapon if necessary. Check the back seat before you indicate which car is yours.

6. Act confident and alert.

7. Wear clothes and shoes that give you freedom of movement.

8. Plan ahead what you would do if attacked. The more you've thought ahead, the more likely you'll act in the way you've planned.

If Attacked:

1. Trust your instincts.

2. Don't be afraid to make a scene, even if it's someone you know.

3. Remain as calm as possible—use your imagination and good judgment to get out of your situation.

If You Are a Victim:

If you become a victim of sexual assault, you will be forced to make a lot of difficult decisions. The first decision is whether or not to report the crime to the authorities. No matter what you decide, rape-crisis experts recommend the following:

1. Don't shower, bathe, or douche before seeking medical attention.

2. Seek immediate medical attention from a doctor or a hospital emergency room. Serious injuries aren't always evident. Insist on tests for pregnancy and venereal disease.

3. Take care of your emotional needs. Check your local phone book for the listing of the nearest rape-crisis center or crisis hot line. Find out what counseling is available in your area. If nothing is available locally, call (202) 333-RAPE, twenty-four hours a day, seven days a week.

4. You have the right to ask questions of the police, doctors, attorneys, and counselors.

5. You have the right to be treated in a kind and sensitive manner by the above persons.

6. After a rape, it is normal to feel fear, anger, loneliness, and helplessness.

7. It is also normal for some victims to act nonemotional and nonfeeling, while others become hysterical. It's normal to cry.

8. Remember, you have the right to do nothing or to report the crime to the authorities and to press charges.

Information for Men:

Legal definition of rape: "An event that occurs without the victim's consent, involved the use of force or the threat of force, and involved sexual penetration of the victim's vagina, mouth or rectum" (National Women's Study).

What Can a Man Do?

1. Stop believing the myths popularized by Hollywood and secular therapists regarding sex.

Myth #1. There's something a little "strange" about the guy who chooses not to have sex before marriage.

Reality #1: AIDS and other equally devastating diseases have given men and women ample reason to save the wedding night for the honeymoon. A wise woman will demand that her husband-to-be is as pure as she.

Myth #2. A man's libido, once inflamed, is as impossible to

stop as a train without brakes, careening down a hill.

Reality #2: That's nonsense! If you have any doubts, imagine yourself in the following situation. You are making out on your girlfriend's sofa. Just as you pass the mythical "point of no return," her father walks in the front door. Could you stop? God created men in His image, not degenerative wimps originating from apes.

Myth #3: Women secretly want to be "raped." When a woman says No, she means Yes.

Reality #3: The law says sexual intercourse becomes rape the moment the victim says No.

Myth #4: If I spend money on her on a date, I have a "right" to demand intercourse.

Reality #4: What rock did you crawl out from under? Any decent woman will tell you that's prostitution. People who respect others do not coerce them into doing things they do not want to do, not a casual date, not a steady boyfriend, not a fiancé, and most certainly, not a husband. Without respect, love cannot survive. And as a prominent psychologist once wrote, "Sex without love is about as satisfying as a good sneeze."

Myth #5: If a woman is sexually active, her date has a "right" to expect her to "put out" for him.

Reality #5: There is no such amendment in the laws as "earning the right" or "being entitled" to sex on a date. Look at it this way; if you left your keys in your car and someone stole it, would you report the theft, or would you shrug and say, "Oh, well, I asked for it"?

Myth #6: Women claim rape out of guilt or spite.

Reality #6: False charges of rape are no more frequent than false charges for any other crime. The degradation and humiliation that follows when a woman reports a rape would deter even the most embittered female from filing a false report.

Myth #7: Rape is hard to prove. It's just her word against mine.

Reality #7: Not anymore. Two new types of evidence are being admitted in the courts. One is "genetic fingerprinting," the process of comparing the DNA makeup of hair or body fluid specimens collected from the victim's body after the assault. These are used to identify the assailant. The other type of evidence is medical testimony as to the presence of "rape trauma syndrome." Symptoms of rape trauma syndrome include intense feelings of degradation, humiliation, guilt, shame, anger, and the need for revenge. This leads to the development of sleep disorders, depression, and phobias.

2. Avoid the chance of becoming involved in dangerous situations. Don't assume that, when things heat up, it's the woman's place to stop you. Take responsibility for your own actions. Apply the same rigorous training to strengthening your emotional and spiritual muscles as you do to build up your mental and your physical muscles.

3. Analyze your own behavior. Anger is a secondary emotion that springs from any one or combination of the following: fear, hurt, or frustration. Go through the list of suggestions given for women and decide what kind of date risk you might be. If you have problems in any of the areas, get professional counseling.

4. Plan ahead. Plan your dates so as not to have long spans of time together in solitude. Make it a policy to only date women whom you respect. And even if a date demonstrates she's not what you thought her to be, respect yourself enough not to compromise your personal values. Sex is a social act. The way we treat one another involves values and character.

5. Review the story of Jesus. Look for dating guidelines. He came to earth to be our example. How did He treat people, women in particular? One general principle comes through all of His personal encounters. Read the story in Luke 8:26-39. When the people of the region told Him to leave their country, what did He do? He left. Jesus never forced Himself on anyone. He was always a gentleman. This should be a Christian man's first line of defense.

For More Information

BOOKS:

Bode, Janet. *Rape: Preventing It, Coping With the Legal, Medical, and Emotional Aftermath*. New York: Impact Books, 1979.

Parrot, Andrea, Ph.D. *Coping With Date Rape and Acquaintance Rape*. New York: Rosen Publishing Group, Inc., 1988.

Storaska, Frederic. *How to Say No to a Rapist—and Survive*. New York: Random House, 1975.

Warshaw, Robin. *I Never Called It Rape*. New York: Harper Collins, 1988.

PAMPHLETS:

Johnson, Kathryn M. *If You Are Raped*. Holmes Beach, Fla.: Learning Publications, Inc., 1984.

McEvoy, Alan, W., and Jeff B. Brookings. *If She Is Raped: A Guidebook for Husbands, Fathers, and Male Friends*. Holmes Beach, Fla.: Learning Publications, Inc., 1991.

"For Safety's Sake: Your Personal Safety Handbook at

UCSD." Student Safety Awareness Program, Undergraduate Affairs/Special Services Center, University of California, San Diego.

MAGAZINE ARTICLES:

Elizabeth Karlsburg. "Acquaintance Rape: What You Should Know." *Teen* (November 1992).

Robbi Sommers. "A Victim's Revenge." *Redbook* (October 1992), 78.

James N. Bond. "Date Rape." *Cross and Crescent* (Summer 1992), 7.

Susan Ince. "New Treatment for Rape Victims." *Glamour* (August 1992), 142.

Donna Christiano. "Rape: Do Your Fears Fit the Facts?" *Glamour* (August 1992), 140.

"Rape Is on the Rise Nationwide, New Federal Crime Survey Reveals." *Jet* (May 1992), 14.

Eloise Salholz and Michael Mason. "Sex Crimes: Women on Trial." *Newsweek*, 16 December 1991, 22.

Roberta Robertson. "A Story of Rape." *Essence* (April 1992).

Andrea Gross. "The Truth About Rape." *Ladies' Home Journal* (September 1992), 42.

"Unsettling Report on an Epidemic of Rape." *Time*, 4 May 1992, 15.

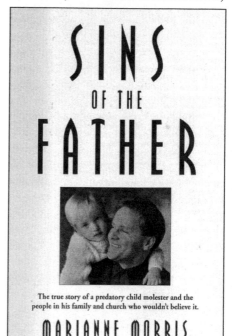

Swept away to another time
The Chloe Mae Chronicles
by Kay Rizzo

Never before have you shared the power of a dream or the emotions of young love as you will in this memorable early-pioneer series.

As Chloe Mae flees from her father's iron rule, she starts down a path of experience she never bargained for. Silence turns to love and tragedy turns to forgiveness as Chloe Mae lifts her heart to God for strength to face whatever life brings.

Four-book set: *Flee My Father's House, Silence of My Love, Claims Upon My Heart,* and *Still My Aching Heart.*

Paper. US$10.95/Cdn$15.35 each. US$34.95/Cdn$48.95 set.
Prices subject to change without notice.

Available at your local Christian bookstore, or call toll free 1-800-44PRESS.

Books You Just Can't Put Down
from Pacific Press

Why is this happening to me, God?

Nowhere to Turn

by Rhonda Graham

Ellen's blank stare followed her husband's figure as he walked out of the house and out of her life. Her head pounded with the same questions over and over. How could this be happening to a pastor's wife? To someone who "played by the rules"?

Nowhere to Turn shares the emotions of a woman going through the pain of divorce and offers hope to Christians enduring crises of faith and family.

US$9.95/Cdn$13.95. Paper.

Available at your local Christian bookstore, or call toll free 1-800-44PRESS.

Prices subject to change without notice.